Chapter 1

1942

The last memory Polly had of Geoff would stay with her for the rest of her life. If only she knew then what she knew now. So many things she would've said and many things she would have done differently. But that's all it was, thoughts. No actions could be taken, her future was already written.

2010

There was something special about Amsterdam, Naomi couldn't help but look around and imagine the history behind each individual building. People using bicycles as the main means of transport around the city, created thoughts of a simpler time. Each bike was dressed in its own personality which reflected the owner.

"What story are you imagining now daydreamer?" Clara asked rolling her eyes but smiling at the same time.

"Oh, nothing I'm just sad our holidays coming to an end, we're definitely going to have to bring mom here one day, she'd love it!" Naomi replied.

Clara responded in the way that Naomi knew she would.

"I don't think she'd like the weed smoking part of it! But I agree, I'm surprised she's never been, considering grandma lived here at one point!"

Naomi had never really thought of that but hearing it made her think. Why had her grandma not visited since or even spoke about Amsterdam much? It was such a beautiful place; it probably wouldn't have had the same affect during the second world war though she thought.

The twin sisters spent their last hour in the Dutch city eating a Nutella pancake before catching a taxi to the airport for their flight home.

Schiphol Airport was probably the biggest airport they'd been to on their tour of Europe.

Their mom had text them about hundred times saying she couldn't wait for them to be home. Despite them only being away for a month she said it had felt like years.

The hustle and bustle that comes with every airport trip was well on its way. Clara had already had a full-on meltdown in the taxi ride, thinking she'd lost the passports, she was holding them the entire time.

Both sisters were very close, but they couldn't be more different. While Clara was the organised one with a clear plan for the future, Naomi was laid back and still didn't really know what she wanted to do with her life.

They'd been together every day for the past 19 years, but the end of this trip also meant the end of their inseparableness.

Clara had a place confirmed at Liverpool University studying law, where she would also be moving to in a few days' time. On the other hand, Naomi had no idea what to do. Her parents had hoped she'd follow in her sister's footsteps but that just wasn't realistic.

Naomi's dream was to be an actress, she'd always been the lead role in the school play and making up performances with Clara from the age of four, much to Clara's delight but she always went along with it.

Neither of them had spoken about Clara moving away for the entire trip. It was as if it wasn't really happening, but as soon as they landed at Birmingham Airport, reality hit home, and they knew they could no longer pretend it wasn't real.

Security checks were complete, and the girls made their way to the first car park where their mom had said she would be waiting.

The British weather never fails to make you wish you were back on holiday. The summer was officially over with the cold chill already snapping in time for September.

Naomi was looking round for her mom when she saw multiple people being dropped off to start their holidays. That's always the worst part when the realisation set in that yours is over.

"Not like mom to be late, she's probably been tracking our flight for the last three hours," Clara said mid yawn.

The twins perched on their suitcases while they waited for their mom.

45 minutes later and they were still waiting.

"Right, now I'm starting to worry, moms like me if I'm not somewhere early then something is wrong." Clara said, pacing up and down.

"Just chill I'm sure everything is fine; the traffic is always hectic at this time." Naomi replied, but deep down she was worried herself, despite being the laid back one.

After ringing their mom multiple times, a man wearing a smart, black suit started running towards them shouting their names.
"Dad?" Clara said looking confused.

"Sorry girls, I tried ringing you, but my phone died, I'm parked in another car park. Want me to carry anything." Their dad asked looking out of breath after running for what looked like miles.

"Where's mom?" Clara asked looking concerned.

"Your grandma Polly's had a fall so your moms at the hospital with her. She wanted to ring you, but she was in a faff, you know what she's like, so I offered to pick you up instead. The cars a bit of a walk I'm afraid, you know I hate these car park charges." Their dad replied, still sounding out of breath.

Shock, their dad was on around £55,000 as a lawyer at a top firm and he was still tight.

The walk seemed to take forever, the girls were shattered, and all Naomi could think about was getting into bed, but she was worried to death about her grandma Polly. They'd always had a strong bond.

"So, I take it you've had a great time then?" Their dad asked once they'd finally got in the car.

"Yeah, lovely thank you, we will have to show you some photos when you drop us off," Clara replied.

"I heard Amsterdam was your favourite place Naomi. Maybe we could all go together one day eh?" Their dad asked sounding hopeful.

Silence filled the car. Naomi turned her head to look outside the window focusing on the traffic.

"Come on Naomi, you can't stay silent forever, we spoke about this. I thought you were going to give dad a second chance?" Clara said turning around from the front passenger seat to look at her.

"You're right Neil sorry, maybe we could've all gone together as a family, but you decided to shag your secretary!" Naomi angrily responded.

Silence once again filled the car, and their father stared straight ahead focusing on the road.

It may have been a year since their Dad had had an affair, but the wound was still wide open, for Naomi anyway. Somehow Clara had managed to forgive him, but Naomi held a massive grudge and only called him by his name, much to his disappointment.

Their mom, Katherine walked in on Neil and his secretary, Stacey, doing the deed in his office, on what seemed like a normal Tuesday afternoon. She filed for divorce straight away.

Even though their mom told the girls that their marriage had ended a long time before he "shagged the slut" (word for word what she said), Naomi refused to even be in the same room as her father, so you can see why the car journey is so awkward.

The 45-minute car journey back home to Worcester seemed to take hours, with the amount of tension. The twin's father hadn't spoken a word since Naomi's outburst and neither of the girls felt like speaking to each other. What a way to end the trip of a lifetime they both thought.

Chapter 2

It was 7pm by the time they got home and despite only having a short flight both girls were ready for bed. They still hadn't said a word to each other at 10pm when their mom arrived home looking stressed and worn out.

"Ah girls I'm so glad your home, sorry I couldn't pick you up but I'm sure your dad explained why." Their mom said bursting in the living room where the twins were catching up on their social media.

"How's grandma?" They both asked in sync.

"Well, she's had a stroke…but it was a minor one and the doctors have said she will make a full recovery in due course. She's still Grandma Polly moaning about the hospital food and making jokes. We can all go and see her tomorrow if you like, I know she's desperate to see you both." Mom said, while putting her feet up.

"Bloody hell, poor grandma. dad only said she'd fallen over." Clara responded looking stressed.

"Well, we all know Dad's not one for telling the truth, is he?" Naomi interrupted sarcastically. She knew it wasn't the right time, but her tiredness had turned into moodiness.

The next morning, Naomi's alarm started ringing at 9am and she'd snoozed it about 10 times before finally getting into shower at 10:30am.

The smell of bacon and sausage filled her nose as she was walking towards the kitchen.

"Morning Miss moody, have we cheered up yet?" Mom asked smiling with the motherly glint in her eye.

"Yes, I was just tired and worried about grandma that's all, sorry for causing a scene. Is Clara still in bed?" Naomi asked feeling guilty over her antics.

"No worries love, I know there's a lot going on at the moment. She got up early to go and meet some friends to say goodbye, before we take her to Liverpool on Saturday. She's going to meet us at the hospital to

see grandma at 1'o'clock. Fancy a bacon and sausage sandwich?"
Mom asked while putting the kettle on.

Shit. It really was only 3 days until Clara went away to university,
Naomi thought. After everything that happened yesterday, she'd
actually forgot, or maybe her mind just blocked it out because she
didn't want to face reality.

The 10-minute drive to Worcester Royal Hospital from their house
soon came round, and Naomi had a strange feeling. A wave of worry
came over her about seeing her grandma. She'd always been a strong
wise woman so to see her in a hospital bed just felt alien to Naomi.
She didn't know what to expect, what if she was different?

"I know that little head of yours, I can tell your worrying. Grandma is
still grandma, she's not going to be any different, so no need to be
scared." Mom said while they walked through the main entrance
doors.

It was as if she read her mind exactly. Naomi knew deep down that her
mom was right, but there was still a part of her that had doubts.

They entered the Laurel 2 ward where Clara was waiting. The twins smiled at each other and Clara put her arm around Naomi with a reassuring embrace. She could tell just by looking at Naomi how she was feeling.

Maybe it was a twin thing, or Naomi was just easy to read. Nevertheless, they always had each other's back, even when one of them was being a bitch.

"We're here to see Polly Madden, she was admitted last night, but I'm not sure if her room has changed." Their mom asked the nurse on reception.

While the nurse checked her computer, Naomi's nerves had settled, and she felt less worried.

The three of them were directed to their grandmas' bed where she was chatting to the female patient next to her.

"Here they are my gorgeous granddaughters, come on sit down. I want to hear all about your trip." She said smiling ear to ear.

Mom was right, nothing could change grandma not even a minor stroke bless her, Naomi thought smiling.

The girls filled their grandma in on everything about their trip even the handsome French boys they met in Paris, Connell and Jasper.

"Wow even I didn't get that much information!" Their mom laughed once the girls had finished talking about their adventures.

An hour passed and Grandma Polly was starting to get tired even though she would never admit it.

"Well, I think we should make a move girls, so we can let you rest mom," Mom said sounding exhausted herself.

"Oh, don't be daft Katherine, I'm fine! I could talk to you girls all day," Grandma replied stifling a yawn.

"I know mom but doctors' orders, and besides Clara needs to finish packing for Liverpool remember." Their mom said reassuringly.

A pang of anxiety rushed over Naomi and for the first time ever, everything just felt too real. With Clara moving to Liverpool, it felt like half of Naomi would go with her. Her confidence all of a sudden flatlined and she felt lost for the first time in her life.

"Right yes of course, well you must come and see me before you leave young Clara," grandma said sternly.

"Definitely grandma, I'd never leave without saying goodbye first," Clara responded with what sounded like sadness in her voice.

They all gave her a hug and began to leave the hospital.

"For an eighty-six-year-old woman she certainly hasn't lost her humour or cheekiness," a man in what looked like a doctor's uniform laughed.

"Ah Doctor Blake isn't it? She certainly hasn't, my mother's made of something else I tell you! Thank you so much for looking after her, I'm very grateful." Mom said sounding genuine.

"Oh definitely, and please call me Fabian! I see you've brought your daughters with you. Your mom was telling me you've been visiting parts of Europe. Best to while you're young I tell you; travelling was the best thing I ever did."

"It really was a wonderful experience." Clara replied smiling.

Naomi was glad she had. Despite loving to perform Naomi always seemed to lose the ability to speak when it came to strangers. But there was something familiar about Fabian. Maybe he was on the ward when she had broken her leg, but she couldn't fully remember.

"Well, we better get going, the car park ticket is almost up! Thank you again," mom said in a rush.

"So, who fancies a McDonalds? My treat." Mom asked while they walked to the car.

She knew the answer before she asked and before long, they were at the drive thru.

Chapter 3

It was 9pm and they all sat down to watch an episode of Luther. It was nice for the three of them to be together again. Even though Naomi's anger towards their dad overtook her being able to think straight, she missed the four of them being a family.

The laughs they used to have when they took the piss out of each other was just a normal evening for them. Naomi never imagined her parents would get a divorce but to many of her friends it was just normal.

They all said she was lucky that her parents could still have a civil conversation, most of their parents couldn't be in the same room together without world war three breaking out.

The episode had finished, and Clara put their favourite show on, F.R.I.E.N.D.S, which they never got tired of.

"Right, I'll leave you girls to it I'm off to bed. Busy day of packing tomorrow Miss Clara. Goodnight." Their mom said as she began walking up the stairs.

Naomi looked over at Clara, who was staring blankly at the screen.

"You okay?" Naomi asked feeling concerned.

"Yeah. I'm just thinking maybe I shouldn't go to Liverpool with grandma being in hospital and everything. What use am I going to be 120 odd miles away, if something bad happens and grandma gets worse?" Clara asked looking helpless.

Naomi suddenly felt a weight lift off her shoulders at the thought of her twin sister staying at home. But she knew she was only being selfish if she agreed with Clara. Mainly because she knew Clara should go away and it was what she wanted, but also because it would be good for them both to do different things.

"Everything will be fine Clara, you've wanted to study law for as long as I can remember, and there's no way mom, dad or grandma would let you stay for that reason. You know if anything happens, you'll be the first to know and I'd come and pick you up myself!" Naomi replied, knowing she'd said the right thing.

"You're right, ah I'm just being silly, and overthinking again. Promise me one thing though, you'll try and make amends with dad? I know it's not easy, but everyone makes mistakes and I know you'll regret it if you don't. You're just being stubborn as usual." Clara laughed rolling her eyes.

Naomi knew she was being stubborn but the thought of their dad cheating on their mom with 'slutty Stacey' still made her physically sick. Maybe she could forgive, but she'd never forget him breaking up their family.

"Fine I'll try but I'm not promising anything!" Naomi replied laughing.

The twins snuggled up on the sofa together while they watched their favourite film Legally Blonde. Both realising this would probably be the last time for a while.

Chapter 4

7am Saturday soon came round, the car was packed bursting with the contents of Clara's bedroom and mom was ready with tissues and coffee to go.

"I can't believe one of my baby girls is off to university! Who'd of thought it eh. I'm so proud of you Miss Clara!" Mom said, bursting with pride.

Cue the disappointment of twin number two, Naomi thought. Her and Clara had had a massive heart to heart last night, and she actually felt positive for once, until she realised, she never would have the intention of going to university.

"Thanks mom, I'm kind of nervous but I'm sure I'll be fine once I've settled in," Clara replied, wiping the sleep from her eyes.

"Exactly, six months remember! You've got to give anything you try at least six months before making a decision about it. You know I'm very proud of you too Naomi. University isn't for everyone, remember what your grandad Madden used to say: You only get one life, don't waste it trying to be a sheep!" Mom laughed trying to sound like grandad himself.

Their grandad had passed away two years ago, but they all thought of him most days. His strong personality shone in every room he entered.

Naomi rolled her eyes as she picked up her iPad for the journey to Liverpool.

"Right let's get going, your dads outside waiting, hopefully he's got the heating going its bloody freezing!" Mom said placing her handbag over her shoulder.

"What? Dads taking us. Unbelievable!" Naomi huffed angrily.

"Oh, for god's sake Naomi, for once this isn't all about you. Dad wanted to take me to university, that's always been the plan regardless of everything that's happened. So put your differences aside and pretend to get on for one day, for me at least!" Clara snapped back.

Clara was right, but Naomi was still annoyed it had been kept a secret from her. Nevertheless, she picked up her bag and followed her mom and sister out the front door into the dark, frosty morning.

Traffic seemed quiet on the motorway for a Saturday morning. The sun was starting to rise and for Naomi it was nice to be up this early in the morning.

Clara had fallen asleep whilst listening to music, she'd been stressing last night so hadn't got much sleep.

Surprisingly mom and dad were talking and laughing like they'd used to, before they separated. Naomi couldn't help but wonder if something had happened between them while her and Clara were away.

Naomi imagined most kids would want their parents to get back together, but she didn't for some reason. She didn't trust her dad to not do the same thing again, and she definitely wasn't prepared to listen to her mum cry herself to sleep again.

They stopped at a garage halfway for a toilet stop. Clara finally woke up and her and Naomi got some fresh air together.

"Do you think mom and dad are going to get back together?" Naomi asked Clara curiously.

"What? No, what makes you think that?" Clara replied laughing.

"Come on, you can't say you haven't noticed them getting along surprisingly well? Moms even laughing at dads' stupid old jokes again." Naomi said as if it was obvious.

"Oh, they're definitely getting along better. But I think they've just come to terms with reality. They'll always have love for each other, but it's clear there not in love with each other. I think they're just being normal for today, for the sake of both of us." Clara casually replied.

"Come on girls, we better get back on the road," dad shouted from the car.

Maybe Clara was right, but Naomi knew there was more to it. She had an instinct, and she was right 90% of the time.

Another hour passed and they arrived at the halls where Clara would be living in for her first year of uni. There was definitely a buzz about the place, but Naomi still couldn't understand why it seemed to be everyone's dream to go to university.

One of her best friends Zoey started an apprenticeship just under a year ago, and she was already in a position to put a deposit down on a house. Her parents were quite well off but even so, Naomi believed you could do just as well if not better if you didn't go to university.

They all picked up a few things to carry out of the car and into Clara's shared accommodation. She'd already been in touch with some of her flat mates and she said they seemed nice, but you never know until you properly meet them, she'd said.

That was another reason Naomi never wanted to go to university, imagine living with five other people who you just couldn't get along with no matter what, that would be a nightmare she thought.

Clara always said she wasn't bothered and that she was there to get a degree in law, making friends would just be a bonus.

Once mom had collected the keys, they entered her accommodation and were greeted by a blonde, tall surfer looking guy. His white teeth beamed against his tanned skin and shaggy hair.

"Good day, you must be the lovely Clara! I'm Josh, nice to meet you." He said smiling as he put out his hand for Clara to shake.

Was that an Australian accent Naomi heard? She thought to herself, why would you ditch the beautiful sandy beaches down under for the bleak blighty weather here in the UK?

"Lovely to meet you too, I've got a lot of stuff I'm afraid to get sorted but I can't wait to meet you all properly soon!" Clara said blushing.

Naomi knew when Clara fancied someone it was so obvious! That was another good thing about the twins they both had completely different taste in men so there were no arguments there.

Naomi definitely thought Josh was fit, there was no doubt about that, but he just wasn't her type.

"Not a problem my love! I'll give you all a hand!" Josh said while taking boxes off mom and dad and trying to mimic a British accent which didn't really work.

Once they'd finally emptied the car, it was time for the hardest part. The inevitable goodbye.

Mom had already got through a whole packet of tissues while she was placing some family photos on Clara's new bedroom wall.

Naomi on the other hand, had been biting her lip multiple times to stop herself from breaking into floods of tears.

"Well guys the moment you've all been waiting for. You've finally managed to get rid of me!" Clara laughed while wiping away a tear that had been brewing for a while.

"Aw come here you. Let's have one final group hug, I think we all need it. Come on Neil and Naomi, for Clara please?" Mom pleaded to them both.

The hug lasted for at least 5 minutes before they all realised it was starting to get dark, and they should get going. Dad didn't particularly like driving in the dark, but he had got better over the years.

"We'll give you girls a couple of minutes while I warm up the car," dad said mid shiver. The temperature had definitely dropped but Naomi felt paralysed with anxiety and sadness at the thought of being apart from her twin.

"Well sis this is it, the time has come to say goodbye…," Clara started singing to lighten the mood.

Both girls burst into laughter which soon descended into tears.

"I don't think I've ever cried so much in one day! But it all seriousness sis, we're both going to be fine. Before you know it, I'll be back home for Christmas and we'll be fighting over a box of Quality Streets!" Clara cried reassuringly.

"Very true, it'll be weird for a while but I'm sure I'll get used to it. At least you've got surfer boy to keep you company," Naomi smirked.

"I don't know what you're talking about!" Clara laughed, but she knew exactly what Naomi meant.

The girls said their last goodbye, and Naomi made her way to the car, while Clara took a slow walk back to her accommodation.

Naomi slept most of the journey home, she felt emotionally drained.

It was just after 8pm when they got home.

"Night dad thanks for taking us," Naomi said without really thinking about it, but she felt so much better for it.

Mom and dad both looked at each surprised but smiling at the same time.

"Night love, let me know if you'd like to go for lunch sometime next week eh?" Dad replied looking relieved.

"Sounds good, I'll text you." Naomi replied as she got out the car.

The house already felt empty just stepping in the door, but Naomi knew this was going to be a good thing. She needed to gain her own independence and find something that she enjoyed.

"Feels strange doesn't it, but we'll soon get used to it love. That was good of you before with your dad. I know it's been difficult but maybe this could be a fresh start for us all. What do you say?" Mom said while she put the kettle on.

"Yeah, you're right. Speaking of fresh starts I'm going to start job hunting, Clara's inspired me!" Naomi said as she did a sarcastic twirl around the kitchen.

"Good for you love. I'm going to have a cuppa and then read a book in bed. We'll go and see grandma tomorrow if you'd like? I'm hoping she'll be discharged in the next couple of days. At this rate I'll have to re-mortgage the house to pay for the parking!" Mom joked.

Naomi lay on the sofa with a steaming cup of tea in one hand and a pack of chocolate biscuits in another. You couldn't beat the combination she thought, especially as the weather was getting colder.

As she scrolled through Indeed looking for jobs, she felt hopeless. There was nothing she found that caught her eye or that she was even remotely interested in.

If only an advert said, 'Blonde 19-year-old girl wanted for a main movie role in Hollywood.'

But that just wasn't realistic she thought. If she'd had gone to stage school from a young age maybe she'd be living a completely different life right now, but things don't always work out that way.

Chapter 5

"Naomi! Come on sleepy head, we need to be at the hospital for 11. You'll have to grab some breakfast from the café."

Naomi sleepily rolled out of bed with a grunt. It felt like she hadn't even been asleep properly. She'd been up most of the night tossing and turning. She knew she shouldn't have drunk that tea right before bed. But she'll never learn.

The end of September was already biting with the chill in the air. It was Naomi's favourite time of year, the dark nights, Halloween, bonfires and best of it all, Christmas. Her mom and dad couldn't understand, they said the Summer was much better with the longer days but Naomi and Clara both disagreed.

"You spoke to Clara much?" Mom asked as they pulled off the drive.

"Yeah, just been texting. She went out last night for freshers. Sounds like she had a good time." Naomi said still barely awake.

"Aww good, seems like she's got a good set of housemates, much better than my experience!" Mom laughed

She'd probably told this story a thousand times at least, Naomi thought on their way to the hospital. All her flat mates partied 24/7, music blaring constantly, and they never once cleaned up. But she met dad in the middle of it, so she'd always said it was worth it for that reason.

"Oh, here they are. Oh, Katherine I can't wait to get out of this place, please tell me you've come to take me home. I had cottage pie last night and I swear it went straight through me. Even your fathers cooking was better than this place and that's saying something!" Grandma said with a frustrated look.

"Oh, mom too much information. I need to speak to the doctor first but if you can, then I will take you home don't worry."

While mom went to find a doctor, Naomi sat down next to her grandma's bed.

"You're missing her aren't you. I know exactly how you feel, it was awful when my twin George died. The family was never the same again. I felt like a piece was missing, I still do if I'm honest." Grandma said with a sad look in her eye.

"I never knew you had a twin grandma! How come you've never said?" Naomi asked shocked.

"Oh well you see I don't really like to remember my life back then. It was a different time; you girls don't realise how lucky you really are!" Grandma said sternly.

"What do you mean? Surely your life in Amsterdam was good, that was my favourite place on the trip, it's so pretty."

As those words trickled out of Naomi's mouth, she saw the colour drain from her grandma's face. She had never seen this expression on her face before.

Just as Naomi was about to ask more questions, her mom, and a doctor she hadn't seen before were standing at the bedside.

"Ah finally, so can I be discharged today doctor? No offence to you, but I'd much rather be at home eating my own food." Grandma asked as her expression went back to normal.

"No offence taken Ms Madden, but I'm afraid it isn't as simple as that." The doctor said looking concerned

Mom had the same concerning expression that Naomi couldn't work out.

"Naomi sweetheart why don't you go and grab a coffee or something from the café. The doctor just needs to speak to us." Mom said in a whisper which Naomi couldn't quite work out.

"Oh, don't be so ridiculous Katherine, she's 19 for god's sake. I'm sure whatever it is, she's going to find out one way or another. Now would somebody just tell me what the hell is going on?" Grandma frustratingly cried.

"Right. I'm afraid Ms Madden on one of the scans that we did after you'd had your stroke, we have found a tumour on your brain.

Unfortunately, it is not in a place where we would be able to operate. There is obviously treatment that you could have which could shrink it slightly. I know this is a lot to take in, but I can give you time to discuss options with your family if you'd like?" The doctor said, looking emotional himself.

Naomi looked over at mom whose eyes were firmly placed on the floor, holding back tears.

"Right. Well. Okay. I wasn't expecting that, that's for sure! But I don't want treatment thank you very much. I've lived a good life, brought up a wonderful daughter who has given me two beautiful granddaughters. What more could a woman ask for eh?" Grandma said smiling, but Naomi could tell she was holding back a flood of tears.

"Wait mom, we need to talk about this. Treatment could give you a longer and better chance of surviving." Mom said in desperation as she took grandma's hand.

"I know sweetheart, but I'd much rather live the rest of my days treatment free surrounded by my family. I don't want hospital appointments here and there when I could be doing something better with my time left. This is my decision remember?" Grandma said as she gripped moms' hand tighter.

"How long if she doesn't have treatment? How long will she have to live?" Naomi asked in a croaky voice.

"It really depends, everyone is different. But on average about 12-18 months. I'm sorry I can't give you a more specific answer." The doctor said, placing his clipboard to his chest.

"See, 12 months of making memories with you girls, not hospital appointments!" Grandma laughed with a reassuring nod.

Naomi flung her arms around her loving Grandma while her mom joined, wishing it was all just a nightmare and they were going to wake up in the real world. But that never happened as the women came out of their embrace.

The journey home from the hospital seemed to take forever. The doctor wanted to keep grandma in overnight just for a couple more observations they'd said. Then she'd hopefully be allowed to go home tomorrow.

As Naomi glanced out the passenger window, she'd thought to herself how could she had been on a once in a lifetime trip to coming home to such devastation.

A woman she had admired her entire life. The person who had given a plaster to her after she'd fallen over in the garden, and someone who had always been there to offer wise advice from years of experience.

How was it fair that soon that woman would be taken away from her and all she'd be left with were memories?

"What if Grandma moved in with us? We could sort the downstairs bedroom out and then when you're at work I could look after her. At least then she wouldn't be on her own." Naomi pleaded as she asked her mom while she was driving.

"You know what love, that's a brilliant idea. My heads so fuzzy at the moment I can't think straight, but at least you are. I'll talk to Grandma tomorrow and see what she thinks, I'm sure she'll say yes." Mom said smiling as she turned into our road.

Chapter 6

"No." Grandma said, as mom suggested the idea to her the next morning.

"Oh, come on mom, Naomi thought of it herself and at least we're all together then, it'll be like a long holiday." Mom said trying to convince grandma.

"I'm certainly not being anyone's burden Katherine. I'm quite capable of looking after myself, I quite like my own company if you don't mind." Grandma replied with a stubborn expression.

"Please grandma! You'll still have your own space, and we can watch loads of telly together and bake like we used to when I was little. Please?" Naomi said with her best impression of puppy eyes.

Grandma rolled her eyes as she looked out the window. Naomi often wondered what was going through her head but more so than ever now.

"Fine. But on one condition. I don't want either of you telling young Clara. The last thing I want is for her university experience to be ruined and her coming home because of me. I know her too well, as soon as you tell her she'll be on that first train back to Worcester." Grandma said pointing her finger at both mom and Naomi.

Mom and Naomi had both talked about telling Clara today, but they were dreading it. Naomi knew that Clara would want to know but Grandma was right she'd be back straight away.

Naomi knew that Clara would never forgive her if she didn't tell her, and she knew she'd do the same if it was the other way round. But would she? The way Naomi felt right now, she wasn't sure she would. Clara would want Naomi to continue fulfilling her dreams.

"Mom, Clara has the right to know. She'd never forgive any of us if we didn't tell her. Remember when you told me about your father keeping things from you. You couldn't look him in the eye again, so imagine how Clara would feel?" Mom said looking desperate.

Naomi couldn't help but wonder what went on when her grandma was younger. There was definitely a tense atmosphere in the room and the last time Naomi felt this was when her parents broke the news of them getting a divorce.

"Ah Ms Madden I'm glad I've caught you before you left, I was worried I'd missed you," a male voice said, suddenly bursting Naomi's thoughts.

"Doctor Fabian! How lovely of you to think of me. Looks like I'll be living with my daughter and granddaughter. They don't trust me on my own, an old bird like me." Grandma laughed, but Naomi knew she was only joking.

Her mom seemed to know it as well as she started laughing. The atmosphere quickly changed back to normal, and nobody felt as if they were stepping on eggshells. The Doctor saved the day, literally Naomi thought.

Grandma was discharged and the three generations made their way home to what they all expected would involve some challenging times ahead.

They'd all agreed to tell Clara the full extent of grandma's illness before she came home for Christmas. That way she'd be able to complete her first semester at least, worry free.

"So, nothing's wrong but she's living with you? That doesn't make sense Naomi, somethings wrong isn't it?" Clara said down the phone to Naomi.

It had been a week since grandma had moved in and up until now Naomi had managed the odd message here and there, but she couldn't escape a full grilling any longer.

"No, but well. Oh, Clara everything is fine, grandma was just feeling lonely and well I thought it would be a good idea, with you being at uni and everything. So, how's it going. Any more updates on hot surfer guy?" Naomi asked panicked, she was terrible at lying, always had been.

The last thing she'd heard about Josh, was that they'd shared a heart to heart one night after one too many tequila shots alongside many bottles of prosecco.

"Naomi, I know when you're lying, you're shit at it! Its cancer isn't it? Oh god please tell me it isn't." Clara asked sounding feeble.

Naomi glanced from the kitchen over at mom and grandma who were watching repeats of The Great British Bake off. They were both so engrossed and had no idea what was being said on the phone.

Naomi felt loyal to her grandma and knew it wasn't her news to tell. But she'd also remembered her promise to Clara, not even thinking at the time she'd have to use it.

"Urgh I know. It's a brain tumour and they can't operate on it Clara. They've said roughly 12-18 months, but they can't be sure. I promise we were going to tell you, but grandma wanted you to enjoy your time and uni and not come back for her. We only wanted the best for you. Please don't be angry." Naomi responded trying to sound strong.

Silence. Naomi couldn't hear anything. She knew exactly how Clara felt, shock. Which is what she'd been feeling the more she processed what was going on. At first, it hadn't felt real but having her grandma's presence around her each day, the thought of losing her had built up more anxiety.

Clara hung up without saying a word. Naomi knew she had done the right thing. Either way Clara was going to be hurt but surely her mom and grandma wouldn't be annoyed with her. They'd do the same thing even if they weren't going to admit it.

The next day rolled round and it was Tuesday, so mom was at work. Naomi still hadn't heard from Clara since their phone call, despite texting her a million times.

Naomi had confessed to telling Clara the truth and surprisingly grandma and mom had been fine with it. Grandma was huffy to begin with but she some came round once Downtown Abbey came on.

"Morning lovey fancy pancakes for breakfast? I'm craving them." Grandma said while licking her lips.

"Sure. Why not? I can make them if you like. Naomi asked, even though she knew the answer.

"Oh, don't be daft! Just because I've got the big C doesn't mean I'm incapable just yet." Grandma tutted.

Naomi sat down in the living room while she put This Morning on. Holly and Phil always managed to cheer her up and offered some escapism at least.

The smell of scrumptious pancakes soon entered her nostrils as grandma brought in a plate full of Nutella and strawberries. A perfect combination she thought.

"We had Nutella ones in Amsterdam each day we were there! They're delicious." Naomi said, her mouth-watering.

Just as she'd said it, she'd noticed the same pale look on her grandmas face from the hospital. What was it about Amsterdam that changed her expression so much she'd thought?

"What happened in Amsterdam grandma? You always look so worried every time I mention it." Naomi asked curiously.

Grandma froze mid bite of a strawberry. She glanced over at Naomi as if a realisation had overcome her.

"Well, I suppose we've got nothing else to do today and I've always wanted to tell someone just never found the right time. No better time than when I'm dying, I suppose." Grandma laughed but with a worrying look at the same time.

And just like that Naomi was about to find out something that would change her family forever.

Chapter 7

1939 – London (Polly)

1939 London was a world away from today. It was Sunday 3rd
September, a sunny bright morning which just felt like any normal day
to me.

I woke up to the smell of toast and coffee brewing. My twin brother
George was just returning from his paper round and my little sister
Jane was pestering my mom for something, as per usual.

"Morning sleepyhead. What time do you call this?" My father joked
peering over his daily newspaper.

"Oh, Frank leave her alone. I remember myself at the age of fifteen,
my father having to throw a cold wet flannel at me to prise me out of
bed. It definitely worked but he never liked the bad mood that came
with it I tell you!" My mother laughed as she washed up.

I've never been a morning person, always loved my lie ins, teenager or not. I joined them at the table as I grabbed a glass of freshly squeezed orange juice, a treat.

It was just after 11am by the time I'd finished my breakfast and a commotion appeared to be happening outside. People were shouting some were even crying.

Our neighbour Jenny came running into our kitchen acting like a lost puppy.

"Have you heard the rumours?" She asked in her strong cockney accent.

"What?" My mother asked. I'll never forget the worried look she had on her face.

"They've only gone and declared another bloody war; honestly why can't everyone just get on?" Jenny pleaded as she slumped on one of our kitchen chairs.

A few minutes went by as my mother tried to calm Jenny down with a whiskey, and there it was an announcement on the radio, that would change many people's lives.

As the clock struck 11:15am, Neville Chamberlain made his announcement on the radio stating that war had broken out. We were at war with Germany…

Chapter 8
2010..

Just as Naomi's grandma was getting into her story, the doorbell rang.
Both women jumped a mile, having felt like they'd transported back in
time.

"I'll get it," Naomi said rolling her eyes.

As she approached the door, she couldn't help but wonder what her
grandma was going to tell her. She was scared but excited at the same
time. She couldn't wait to tell Clara, but then she remembered they
weren't talking.

"Hello love, ready for lunch? It's a bit chilly, you might want to wrap
up warm." Dad smiled as he rubbed his hands together trying to warm
them up.

Naomi had completely forgotten she'd made plans for lunch. But she
was looking forward to a change of scenery.

"I thought we'd try the Harvester. Is that okay? I haven't been there in ages." Dad said after Naomi had grabbed her coat and made sure her grandma was okay being on her own.

They always used to go to the Harvester when Naomi and Clara were younger. It was their end of term treat for doing well at school. Those were the good old days Naomi thought.

"Yeah, sounds good," Naomi replied. For once in her life, she felt nervous around her dad. It was like being with a stranger considering she hadn't spoken to him much in almost a year.

It was also the first time they were doing something together just them two. Clara had always been there. They used to call themselves the three musketeers when their mom was working, and dad used to be in-between jobs.

They were good times, and Naomi didn't realise at the time how special the memories would be. She'd taken for granted her family being together, without secrets.

"Your mom told me you haven't spoken to Clara since she found out about grandma. She'll come round love; you did the right thing. I'm sure she'll realise soon." Dad said breaking Naomi's thoughts.

"I hope so, this is the longest we haven't talked, and I hate it." Naomi sulked.

"Yeah, I know what that's like," dad said trying to lighten the mood.

Naomi actually felt guilty for the first time. But then she thought about what her dad did, and he deserved to feel guilty himself, but not forever she thought.

They finally sat at their table after managing to get stuck in horrendous lunch time traffic.

"I bet you're starving, I know I am," dad said looking at the menu.

What shall I have, Naomi thought to herself? She usually went for a pizza, but she fancied something different. May as well push the boat out if dads paying, she thought.

"I think I'll go for the fillet steak, sounds delicious," Naomi said as she caught her dad almost choking on a sip of coke.

"Are you sure love? The pizzas sound nice, you used to love them here. Remember?" Dad asked, looking hopeful.

"Yeah, but I'm sick of having the same thing, good to try new things eh?" Naomi said feeling mischievous. She knew her dad was tight, she was only going to use it to her advantage this time, or maybe a couple more she thought.

Once they'd finished their meal it was 5 o'clock already. Naomi had had a good time considering she felt nervous to begin with. Maybe it was time to forgive him, after all you only get one life, no point living in anger.

"So, how'd you feel about maybe meeting Stacey some day?" Dad asked as they left the pub.

There it was the bombshell. Naomi hadn't even considered her dad would still be seeing the 'secretary.' Maybe her mind had just convinced her so much that her mom and dad were getting back together. Or maybe she just wanted to believe it deep down.

"Um I don't know dad. I think my anger has definitely died down. But I'd rather focus on my relationship with you first if that's okay?" Naomi asked feeling deflated.

"Of course, love, I completely understand. Your mom said she didn't think you would be ready yet. It's absolutely fine." Dad replied looking genuinely okay about it.

"You spoke to mom about it?" Naomi asked confused.

"Only briefly I just wanted to know if I should mention it. Obviously, I never meant or wanted this to ever happen to our family but I'm glad me and your mom are getting on better now and I hope we are too?" Dad asked doubtfully.

"Yeah, I think so. One step at a time eh?" Naomi said nudging her dad as they got into his car.

Dad smiled, and they made their way back home.

"So how was it? I've just put a lasagne in if you fancy some later?" Mom asked curiously just as Naomi walked through the door.

"No thanks I'm absolutely stuffed. Couldn't eat another thing. Might have some pancakes later though if there are any left over." Naomi laughed.

Mom rolled her eyes as she poured them both a glass of squash.

"It went okay, was nice to catch up actually. Have you heard from Clara yet?" Naomi asked changing the subject.

"Good, I'm glad. Yeah, she rang while I was making tea, spoke to grandma and then me briefly. I've told her she can't be angry at you and that it was grandma who didn't want to worry her. I'm sure she'll cool off in a couple of days." Mom replied as she walked into the living room.

Naomi wasn't too worried, she knew her sister, and she was just acting out to make her point. Mom was right she'd be back to normal in a couple of days, well Naomi hoped any way.

"Where's grandma?" She asked as she sat on the sofa.

"She's gone for a lie down. She's fine just exhausted, I think. Been a busy last couple of weeks for her love." Mom replied as she flicked through the channels on the tv.

Naomi knew her grandma needed to rest but she was looking forward to hearing more of her story. Oh well, there's always tomorrow she thought.

Chapter 9

The next morning soon rolled around, Wednesday, hump day Naomi thought. Although with her being at home constantly everyday felt the same. She knew she needed to find a job sooner rather than later.

Naomi rolled on her side to pick up her phone. She'd had four miss calls from Clara and it was only 10am. She rang back immediately.

"Finally, lazy bones! I'm the student partying, it should be me lying in not you!" Clara laughed at the other end of the phone.

"It's not even that late, I've had a busy few days I'll have you know. What's wrong anyway? Didn't think you were talking to me." Naomi asked still felling annoyed that she'd been ignored.

"Oh, nothing I just wanted to say I understand why you didn't tell me about grandma. I've been thinking about it, if it was the other way round. I would've done the same. And I might have a teeny bit of gossip." Clara replied sounding surprisingly chirpy.

"Thank god, you took your time. Go on then do tell." Naomi said still feeling half a sleep but glad her and her sister were back to normal again.

"So, you know surfer Josh. Well, we may be kind of dating. Nothings official but let's just says he's a very good kisser!" Clara squealed down the phone.

"I knew it. I guessed it as soon as I saw you blushing when we first met him. Aw I'm pleased for you clar, you deserve it." Naomi said genuinely pleased, but she couldn't help but feel a bit jealous. Her first boyfriend, Chris cheated on her when she was 17 and she'd never really been able to trust anyone since.

"Thanks sis! I better go anyway got a lecture in 20 minutes, send my love to grandma and mum I'll ring them tomorrow. Bye."

And she was gone. Living her fun student life, while Naomi was sat at home twiddling her thumbs she thought.

She had a quick shower, put her daily make up on and made her way downstairs to find her grandma watching television.

"Morning love, there's a pot of tea in the kitchen if you want one." Grandma said as she tucked into to her toast.

"Thank you has mum been called into work again?" Naomi asked noticing her car wasn't on the drive.

"Yeah, extra agency shift came up at 6 this morning so she decided to go in, think they were short staffed."

Mum worked as a carer at the local nursing home. She only did 3 days a week normally but if agency popped up, she found it hard to say no, Naomi thought.

"So, you going to continue telling me your story today grandma?" Naomi asked once she'd had her breakfast.

"I knew you were dying to ask, saw you hesitating in the kitchen," Grandma laughed.

"Well, no interruptions today hopefully." Naomi said as she remembered her lunch with her Dad yesterday.

"I suppose. Well, I'll tell you my story, if you keep the tea and biscuit supply going." Grandma said smiling.

"Deal," Naomi replied, feeling apprehensive about what she'd find out today.

Chapter 10

London 1939

Polly

The news of war breaking out was something that many people had seen coming for a while. But to me as a 15-year-old it was scary.

Mum continued to potter around the kitchen to keep herself busy while Dad carried on reading his newspaper.

I decided to go to my bedroom. I thought reading would help, it always occupied me and took my mind off things that I was worrying about.

Not long after I finished a chapter, there was a knock at the door, it was George looking white as a ghost.

"I'm going to have to go, and fight aren't I sis?" George asked me, shaking to the core.

"Oh, George come and sit down you fool. Remember that lesson we had in English and fat Liam asked if he'd have to join if a war was to break out? But Sir said no because the age is 18 and 19 if you're in higher education. So, you can continue doing you school certificate exam. No need to worry." I responded trying to calm him down.

I could feel the stress escape his body. He'd always been a stress head and often confided in me. Mum and Dad weren't really talkers, we never felt we could share our feelings much.

Chapter 11

1940

Polly

George and I celebrated our 16th birthday at the beginning of
September 1940. It was very different to what we'd been used to, but
our mother still tried to make it special.

My father was busy working. He was a Police Constable so work
always seemed to take priority.

Jane was centre of attention as usual, demanding sweets and pop,
which we were very limited to, due to rationing.

"I still don't get why Mum never tells her off, she's so spoilt!" I
muttered to George who was sat next to me at the table.

George just laughed, and had the same excuse as he always did, she's
the youngest, and didn't we know it.

'Ahh I don't believe it! I've forgotten the bloody milk. I don't know how; it was top of my list!" My mother screamed from out of nowhere.

"Don't worry Mum I'll go and get some, shops only down the road." George said getting up off his chair.

"No, don't be daft its dark honey, I'm sure we can go without for one night." My mother smiled putting her hand on his shoulder.

"Mum I'm 16 now, I think I can go to shop when its dark for a bottle of milk." George laughed as he put his coat and scarf on.

I nibbled on some cake, while my mother was drying up. Jane had managed to occupy herself by colouring in.

No more than 15 minutes later there was a bang which shook our house, followed by deathly screams which echoed and made me feel physically sick.

I looked over at my mother who looked white with her eyes almost popping out their sockets.

"Quick we need to get to the air raid shelter. Hurry!" Our mother screamed as she grabbed the coats.

"But Mom what about George? I need to go and find him." I screamed almost bursting into tears.

A look of realisation appeared over my mother's face. She looked around the room as she remembered George wasn't there.

"Shit. The bloody milk." She said, running her hand through her hair and looking terrified.

"Right, you go and take Jane to the shelter, and I'll go and look for George. Under no circumstances do either of you leave this house. Do you understand?" Our mother said glaring at me and Jane.

An hour had passed, and neither our mother nor George had returned. I was sat in the air raid shelter freezing, while Jane was fast asleep.

We hadn't heard any more bangs what I assumed had been a bomb, but I felt physically sick. The thought of anything happening to my mother or George made me want to cry.

A short while later, the siren for an all-clear signal sounded, and I felt slightly relieved but a fear of the unknown crept over me.

I picked Jane up and carried her back in the house. It was empty and dark with left-over food from our party on the table and wrapping paper on the floor.

I wanted to go out looking but knew I couldn't leave Jane on her own. I was exhausted but nothing was going to make me sleep until I knew that Mum and George were home and safe.

About an hour later, after trying to distract myself reading, I saw a turn of the front door handle.

Mother followed by my father both walked in looking like a pair of ghosts.

I knew as soon as I saw Mum's tear-stained face and Dad's sombre look that something wasn't right.

I felt my stomach clench as I tried to get words out.

"What's happened? Where's George?" I asked, feeling a lump at the back of my throat.

Mum shakily walked over to me and put both her hands on my shoulder and just looked at me solemnly.

She didn't need to say anything. I knew. George was gone.

I screamed, as I collapsed to the floor still holding on to Mum. I felt like I couldn't breathe as Mum held me tighter as we cried and cried until we no longer had anything left.

Dad stared at the wall, looking empty as if he just didn't know what to say.

Chapter 12

2010

Naomi

Naomi looked at her grandma in disbelief. She couldn't even begin the imagine the pain and shock her poor grandma Polly had had to go through at such a young age.

"Oh, grandma I'm so sorry, it must've been awful for everyone." Naomi said feeling emotional herself.

Polly stared blankly at the ground. The colour had drained from her pink complexion. It had been years since she'd relieved that moment through words. She'd thought about it daily of course but hadn't gone through the stages.

"Why don't we take a break, I'll make us a cuppa and some sandwiches. Loose Women will be on in a bit." Naomi suggested sensing her grandma's sadness.

"Sounds wonderful love." Polly replied.

While Naomi prepared lunch, her phone started ringing. It was Clara.

"Hello," Naomi answered.

"Hi! Fancy opening the front door," Clara said giddily.

"Eh." Naomi replied confused as she unlocked the front door.

"SURPRISE!" Clara screamed with a massive smile on her face. She was standing there in an oversized hoodie, shorts, and a baseball hat, holding what looked like a bag full of washing Naomi presumed.

"What are you doing here?" Naomi asked as the twins hugged for the first time in a month.

"Well, its progress week at uni, basically half term in school language so I thought I'd come home for a couple of days to catch up. You know I love a good surprise," Clara laughed.

The twins sat down with their lunch while their grandma did her sudoku.

Clara had been filling them both in on the lovely Josh. Her smile grew bigger the more she talked about him.

Naomi couldn't wait to meet him properly give him the sister chat. It had always been a joke between them to vet each other's boyfriends. It obviously hadn't worked for Naomi's ex, he still turned out to be a cheat.

Polly had returned to her normal chatty self as she watched her granddaughter with heaps of pride.

"Well, that's enough of my talking! So, what have you two been up to? I heard you made your famous sticky toffee brownies the other day grandma." Clara asked enthusiastically.

"There's still some left I think my love, although your sister had the best pieces," Polly smirked as she glanced at Naomi.

Clara rushed to the kitchen, like a zoo animal during feeding time.

Naomi was hoping her grandma would finish telling her story to the both of them, but she realised she was struggling enough just telling her.

Maybe she should tell Clara, but she didn't want to disrespect her grandmother. It could be something just between the two of them she thought.

The rest of the week was spent shopping and watching tv together, the twins had a lot to catch up on.

On Friday they went for a meal with their mom and dad to nandos, Grandma Polly was supposed to go but she wasn't feeling well so decided to stay at home and rest.

It was weird for them all to be together again but nice at the same time. Naomi no longer saw her parents as a couple but best friends putting their differences aside for the sake of their children.

She definitely wasn't ready to play happy families with Stacey yet, but she could feel herself making progress.

Saturday soon came round which meant it was time for Clara to go back to Liverpool. She was catching the 9:00am train so Naomi walked her to the station which was only 10 minutes from the house, and she didn't have as much luggage this time.

Josh was meeting her at Lime Street station in Liverpool so he could help with her bags.

It had been so nice having her home for a few days Naomi thought, but she was looking forward to hearing her grandma's stories again.

Chapter 13

The crisp autumn leaves were being taken by the wind as Naomi walked home from the train station.

Pumpkins were decorated on the neighbourhood doorsteps in preparation for the trick or treaters.

As Naomi approached her house, her mom was coming out the door in her work uniform.

"Ah I've been called into work again love. Only for a few hours though. There's a beef stew in the slow cooker, you and your grandma help yourself about six." Mom said as she fumbled with her car keys.

Nothing better, Saturday night tv and beef stew in the winter, Naomi thought.

"See you later mom, don't work too hard," Naomi smiled.

"Oooo X factor tonight grandma!" Naomi said as she sat down.

"Oh, I can't stand that show! Simon Cowell, who does he think he is?" Polly replied tutting.

"Its entertainment grandma, that's what it's all about!" Naomi replied laughing.

"Well, I think its rude if you ask me, those poor contestants, being judged on their appearance as well as their voice," Polly replied raising her eyebrow.

Naomi couldn't help but laugh. She loved these conversations with her grandma. Two generations sharing their opinions, you couldn't beat it. It was only light-hearted after all.

"Now, put the kettle on and I'll continue my story," Polly declared looking serious.

London
1940

The next few weeks that followed felt like Groundhog Day. We had George's funeral 2 weeks after his death. It was one of the worst days of my life. Even worse than your grandfathers.

Don't get me wrong, I loved your grandad with all my heart, but he had lived a long, happy life. He'd had children, grandchildren, wonderful holidays and happy memories. But George had all these potential things taken from him in an instant.

I stood next to my sister in the church service, she squeezed my hand so tightly for the entirety. I was the only older living sibling now and I guess I took her under my wing. George had always been better with her, so I thought I owed it to him.

I glanced to the side of me to see and hear mom sobbing in her handkerchief, I don't think she's stopped since she told me the news.

I heard her at night get up, go to the kitchen, and just sit and sob. She hadn't drunk a tea, coffee or ate any cereal with milk in it since. She blamed herself but at the end of the day there was nothing any of us could've done I thought.

My father was a proud man. He rarely showed any emotion, just anger if us kids were playing up. But today at Georges funeral, tears were running down his cheeks, and his eyes were placed firmly on the ground.

"We are gathered here today in deeply unfortunate events but to celebrate the short, but loving life George had. Now please join me with the first hymn." The priest said with a glum look.

I can't remember much of the rest of the service. It's all a bit of a blur. The wake that followed was just as bleak.

Our neighbours all pitched in to make food, which we were very grateful for, but in reality, I think we all just wanted to be alone.

Sombre looks graced me the entire evening. Everyone kept saying to me "we're so sorry," but in reality, I just kept thinking you're just relieved it's not your family member. Ungrateful I know but I felt like I was drowning in grief.

Myself, my mother, father and little sister all cried at various points but not at one point did we ever talk about our feelings. You didn't in those days, you were just expected to get on with it.

A few months passed and things began to feel lighter. There were moments everyday where I just wanted to curl up into a ball and cry, but I wanted to be strong, I needed to be strong.

I just kept picturing the look George had on his face at the thought of having to fight in the war. Pure terror. I imagined it would have been the same look when he died. But there was no point thinking like that.

I started writing a diary, mainly with my feelings. It sort of felt like counselling. I wasn't getting any advice back, but it was still cathartic.

My father came home one evening with a brief case looking disappointed. I couldn't quite work out what the look was. As Jane and I finished our tea he asked us to go to our room for a bit while he spoke to mom.

I must admit I thought the worst. Did he want a divorce, was he ill? All these questions were running through my mind at 80 miles per hour.

An hour had passed, and I'd heard a plate smash, mom shouting and dad trying to calm her down.

I just continued to read my book which helped me block the noise out.

"Polly, Jane can you come downstairs please. Your father and I need to speak to you." My mom bellowed upstairs with a stern tone to her voice.

She really emphasised the word father, which demonstrated her mood towards him as we entered the kitchen.

My parents were stood at opposite ends of the kitchen. Mom's face was looking at dad with daggers, while dad's eyes were placed firmly on us.

"Your father has some wonderful news he would like to share with you, really lifechanging," Mom said sarcastically as she pulled the dining chair out and slumped herself down.

Dad glared at mom in disappointment, I could tell it was something he was hoping she would've supported.

"Work are transferring me to Amsterdam. They need someone to cover intelligence there while monitoring our soldiers who are fighting for our country. It's something I haven't got much choice in I'm afraid, and I understand the timing couldn't be any worse." Dad explained as his shoulders dropped to the floor.

I just stood there; I think I was expecting something worse. If anything, this was nothing compared to hearing about George's death.

"So, you're leaving us?" Jane asked, not fully understanding.

'No of course not sweetheart. You'll all be coming with me; we have accommodation paid for by the force. You can continue going to school and Polly you can do whatever your heart desires." Dad said, looking a little more settled.

Mom sat there and continued to roll her eyes. I could understand why mom was upset because it was a shock. But if I'm being honest, I think we all needed a change of scenery. Our house just held too many memories of George, in every corner, which made grieving even harder.

"How long for?" I asked out of curiosity.

"I don't know love could be a month, could be 12 depends on this blasted war. We'll be leaving in three days though so not much time to pack I'm afraid," Dad responded wiping his brow.

"Sounds good, I'll be glad of the change if I'm honest," I replied, feeling relieved it wasn't anything serious.

Mom looked at me surprised, I think she was expecting me to kick off and put an argument across. But realistically what was keeping me here?

School was no longer safe, neither were the streets. Not that I was expecting Amsterdam to be any safer but meeting new people would be good. That was my take on it anyway, a fresh start.

Chapter 14

Naomi

"Well, all that reminiscing has made me hungry love. Fancy plating up that stew?" Polly suggested mid yawn.

"Sounds good, fancy a glass of pinot grigio?" Naomi smirked as she stretched her legs.

"Oh, go on then, why not?" Polly smiled.

As Naomi dished up the mouth-watering stew, she couldn't help but wonder what her grandma was going to tell her about her time in Amsterdam. But at the same time, she was apprehensive, as her grandma had never spoken about it much, even when her and Clara had booked to go there

Mom rushed in just as Naomi had set her grandma's down on a tray.

"Ooo that was good timing! Wine as well? What's the special occasion love?" Mom asked Naomi as she hung her scarf and coat up. She looked exhausted.

"No reason just fancied one. You go and put your feet up and I'll bring yours out." Naomi replied feeling content.

The rest of the evening was spent watching X Factor and relaxing. A perfect Saturday Naomi thought.

Grandma had gone to bed to read, and mom had fallen asleep on the sofa. So, it was just Naomi flicking through the channels trying to find something decent to watch.

After giving up hope she resorted to repeats of F.R.I.E.N.D.S, it was an easy watch and she never got bored of it.

It was 9am Sunday morning and Naomi was surprisingly wide awake, which was rarity for this time in the morning.

The house was awfully quiet she thought. Her grandma was usually up and about around 8am and she didn't think her mom was working unless she'd been called in again.

As she wondered downstairs to get a coffee and some breakfast, she saw a note on the work service with NAOMI in bold lettering.

'HI LOVE, HAD TO TAKE GRANDMA FOR A CHECK UP AT THE HOSPITAL, JUST ROUTINE COMEPLETELY FORGOT ABOUT IT, YOU'RE GRANDMA KNEW BUT DIDN'T THINK TO REMIND ME! WE'LL BE OUT FOR A COUPLE OF HOURS MIGHT GO INTO TOWN TO GET SOME LUNCH SO PLEASE YOURSELF. GRANDMA HAS LEFT YOU AN ENVELOPE WITH SOMETHING IN IT, DON'T KNOW WHAT IT IS, SHE WAS BEING VERY SECRETIVE. LOL. SEE YOU LATER, MOM XXX.'

That explains it Naomi thought, not like mom to forget things like that but she had been in and out a lot with work lately.

Naomi opened the envelope which had several pieces of paper in filled with her grandmas handwriting, at the top it read:

'Thought I'd right the next bit of my story down for you. Figured I'd be tired after my appointment today. Enjoy, you'll still need the tea and biscuits to go with it.'

Perfect, Sunday was sorted, Naomi thought. She made a coffee and sat down on the window seat in the kitchen and began to read her grandmas words.

Chapter 15
Polly
1940

The next few days resulted in packing, stressing and more packing. My mother had warmed to the idea more now that Jane and I were on board, and her and my father seemed to be getting on better.

A holiday was very rare in my childhood, we weren't poor, but we definitely weren't rich either.

The government were trying to encourage 'Holidays at Home' to reduce unnecessary travel. But the rich were still going regardless.

Only my father had been on a plane before, so this was a very new experience, something I was excited about.

My cousin and his wife were newlyweds, so they were going to rent out our house while were away.

I packed my books, essential clothes, and photos of George, so that he could come with us as well.

My mother kept saying she felt like she was leaving George behind and that it wasn't fair, so I suggested the photo idea, which she loved. I knew that George would want us to continue with our lives anyway and not be sad. He was always the positive one of the family.

"But I want to take my dolls house! I can't leave it here, who's going to feed them all?" Jane screamed from her bedroom sounding spoilt.

"Love, we won't be able to fit it on the plane, I'm sure your father can buy you a brand new one in Amsterdam, as been as he keeps going on about the rise he will be receiving," Mom said with a hint of sarcasm.

The day of our flight soon arrived and to say I wasn't nervous at all would be a complete understatement.

I'd been to the toilet about ten times, my stomach was doing summersaults and my palms were so sweaty I could drink them.

It was mid-October, so autumn was in full swing. We had our hats, scarf and gloves on which made the nervous sweating worse.

We flew from Croydon Airport which had been attacked in an air raid in August, it was very quiet, but we were the only flight on that day.

There was one of my father's colleagues coming as well, but his family had refused to move. I felt sorry for him if I'm being honest, he looked so lost.

The flight took just over an hour, as you know, and the experience itself felt quite joyful. The take-off provided me with the adrenaline rush I needed, and I felt relaxed for the entire journey.

We were landing in Amsterdam at a great time of uncertainty. Nazi Germany were at large of invading in the Netherlands and my father was told that many civilians were fearing the worst.

Part of my father's job was to monitor the situation, report back to England and help in any way that he could. My mother was instructed to stay at home as much as possible, my sister was promised a normal school life and I decided to go with the flow.

There were many news stories floating around in London about the miss treatment of Jews but not quite to the extent that anyone could've ever imagined.

We stepped off the plane to similar weather that we'd left in London. Jane had fallen asleep, so she had to be carried off.

My father was met by two Dutch officers who had a car ready for us so we could get to our new home for the time being.

I never quite realised how high up in the police force my father was, well you don't at that age do you really. But Amsterdam certainly changed my respect for him in more ways than one.

"Mr and Mrs Coldfield pleasure to meet you. I'd like to personally thank you on behalf of the force for relocating. Your help is much appreciated." One of the officers said professionally.

The journey to our 'house' only took about 30 minutes. The streets were practically empty, nothing compared to London. I guess looking back now I was sort of expecting Amsterdam to be normal compared to London, but the extent of the world war effected all countries in different ways. Nobody got off lightly.

Our new neighbours were there to greet is with a fruit basket, as we collected our belongings out of the car. The buildings were very dark and although all houses were joined, they were very narrow. Quite strange if you really focus on it.

Our neighbouring family were The Jansen's': two children, Grace a year older than Jane and Geoff the same age as me and George. Their mother was referred to as Mrs Jansen and their father, Mr Jansen who was also a local police officer.

In May 1940, the Dutch armed forces had surrendered, leaving them in the hands of the German Army. This meant my father and the few fellow police officers that remained were all acting undercover. I didn't know this at the time but was ordered to secrecy as soon as we entered our home.

This sent shivers down my spine. I was terrified and regretted not putting up an argument to come in the first place. But then I thought about my father's colleague who was all alone without his family, and I felt lucky that my father had the three of us around him.

I knew the next however months we were going to be there were going to be difficult, but I had never prepared myself for what was actually going to happen.

Chapter 16
Naomi

Trust grandma to leave it on a cliff-hanger like that, Naomi thought.

While she loved reading her grandmas words there was nothing better than watching her grandma tell her story. The raw emotion that shone through and the way her grandma reminisced, demonstrated this secret that she had hidden for so many years.

Just as Naomi was trapped in her thoughts, her phone started ringing, it was Clara.

"Heyyy!" Naomi answered.

"Hi sis, just checking in. How did grandma get on at her hospital appointment? I've text mom but haven't heard anything back." Clara asked.

"I'm not sure they left early, but they're not back yet. Mom said they might go for some lunch after." Naomi responded as she looked at the time. It was 12pm already, the day was going quick she thought.

She had been so engrossed in her grandmas' story she'd even let her coffee go cold.

"Ahh okay, well just text me later to keep me updated. Josh and I are going to The Cavern in a bit for some drinks and our flatmate is performing there."

The Cavern is a music venue famous for hosting bands such as the Beatles in the 60s. Naomi had never been herself, but Clara couldn't wait to go when she found out she'd secured a place at Liverpool University.

"Yeah of course! Have a lovely time, say hi to Josh for me." Naomi responded getting distracted thinking about what she was going to have for lunch.

After several minutes of contemplating between a tuna sandwich and a toastie. She decided to go for the tuna sandwich.

Football seemed to dominate the Sunday television schedule which Naomi found so boring! A repeat of Keeping up with the Kardashians it was. You can't beat a bit of trashy reality tv she thought.

An hour passed and Naomi heard her mom's car pull up in the drive. She picked up her plates and entered the kitchen to greet them at the door.

Both women walked in looking drained and dishevelled. Moms tear stained face made Naomi's heart drop and suddenly she felt physically sick. Her grandma looked exhausted as if she wasn't really there.

"I think I'm going to have a lie down love, tired doesn't even come close. I'll be up before dinner." Grandma said as she walked towards her bedroom at a slower pace than usual.

"What's happened mom? Was it bad news?" Naomi asked with a squeaky voice. She felt worse than she had when they were at the hospital.

"Only what we should've expected love. Your grandma's tumour has grown slightly which means she'll need more help at home with daily tasks. I think it's just come as a bit of a shock, even though we should've been expecting it soon." Mom said drowsily, she looked so weak Naomi thought.

"Oh, poor grandma. Well, you go and rest mom I'll sort something for tea, might do some baking as well as a little treat for later." Naomi responded feeling useless.

"Thanks love sounds lovely. I think I'll stick a box set on or something. I'm going to take some extended leave off work, so I can be grandma's carer. I've been doing it for years, no point paying a stranger to come in and your grandma seems more comfortable with that idea anyway." Mom said as she grabbed some water and walked into the living room.

Naomi felt like everything was out of her control, which in reality it was. Her grandma had always been so independent, but she was slowly witnessing her deteriorating, and it made her feel so empty.

After a walk to the local shop, her mind felt clearer, and she decided she just needed to focus on the present instead of worrying about the future.

As Naomi entered the kitchen with her ingredients for a chicken stir fry, she thought about her mom being at home all the time and how this would affect her grandma finishing her story.

Would she continue with mom being there? Would Naomi ever find out what has haunted her grandmother all these years? All these questions were running through Naomi's head, but at the end of the day, it was her grandma's choice.

It was soon 7 o'clock and dinner was ready to be served. Naomi had set the table with a bottle of rose and a jug of water.

"Wow, this looks amazing love, maybe you should go down the chef route," mom suggested smiling.

"I wouldn't go that far mom; you haven't tried it yet!" Naomi laughed as she sat down.

"Well, I'm sure it tastes delicious. Your grandmas still asleep I'm afraid so it'll be just me and you," mom said fighting back tears.

Naomi's mom had always been strong, when her emotions got the better of her, she tried to hide away so Naomi and Clara couldn't see the pain she was in when their parents divorced.

But they knew. they helped in any way they could, but deep down they knew she just needed time.

Their grandad had always told them times a great healer, and Naomi knew she would have to keep reminding herself that because of the inevitable in the next few months.

Chapter 17
Naomi

Monday morning soon rolled round, and Naomi's grandma seemed to be feeling much brighter. She was still managing to get dressed in the morning and get breakfast. Naomi knew there were going to be good days and bad days.

"Morning grandma, how you are feeling today?" Naomi asked looking hopeful.

"Much better, thanks love. Did you read my pages?" Grandma asked looking like her normal inquisitive self.

"I did, thank you." Naomi replied smiling.

"Good, well I've sent your mom on a few errands, so we've got time to continue." Grandma said as she got comfortable in her chair.

Amsterdam 1940 November
Polly

It was coming towards the end of November, and we'd completed our first month in Amsterdam.

I would've loved to explore more of the city but that just wasn't possible during the time we were there. I spent most of my time helping Mom with cooking, housework and reading my books.

I occasionally helped mom to home-school Jane, but she was a nightmare. Screaming and throwing tantrums like you wouldn't believe. God rest her soul.

My father had his own work area that we weren't allowed to disturb from 8am to 5pm Monday to Friday. We were constantly reminded his job was very important, more important than our own needs at times.

Sundays were game days. Each week we took it in turns to pick a game we wanted to play. It could be a board game, or it could be made up. Jane's choice consisted of bossing us around for the entire day.

It was Wednesday morning; I'd had breakfast and I was just finishing my diary entry for the previous day.

"Would you mind popping to the shops for me love? We need some bits and bobs for lunch." Mom asked me as she was doing some math sums with Jane, who wasn't paying the slightest bit of attention.

"Okay, I'll just grab my shoes and coat," I replied as I finished writing my last sentence.

"Oh, and check with next door if they want anything, they've done us a few favours these last few weeks." Mom asked, distracted as Jane threw all her pens on the floor.

"Okay." I said rolling my eyes as I walked out the door. I didn't mind helping next door, but I barely knew them, and it was sooo cold outside. I could feel the chill just being inside the house. Our coal fire helped but it was freezing at night.

As I stepped outside, I could see soldiers patrolling the streets. It wasn't illegal to go out, but it felt very surreal compared to living in London.

I approached the Jansen's door and knocked hesitantly. After my second knock the door finally opened.

Mrs Jansen gradually opened the door with a worried look on her face which soon disappeared when she saw me.

Her brown hair was scarped back into a tight bun and over her dress was an apron, covered in flour.

"Hi Polly, excuse the state of me, I'm attempting to make some bread! What can I do for you?" Mrs Jansen asked in her strong Dutch accent.

"I'm just going to the shop and wondered if you needed anything?" I replied feeling shyly.

"Oh, how kind of you! I was just about to send my son Geoff. Why don't you go together keep each other company?" Mrs Jansen said with a massive smile on her face.

Geoff was tall for his age. He had short dark brown hair and piercing green eyes. He was warm and made me feel at ease within seconds of our walk.

Autumnal leaves were dancing along the canal paths in a calming manner.

"So, are you missing London much?" Geoff asked me as we walked over the first bridge. His accent was strong, but his English was incredible. I felt ashamed that my ability to speak another language was non-existent.

"Umm I suppose a little. I haven't given it much thought if I'm being honest," I replied breezily.

I don't really know why I hadn't felt homesick or missed 'home' as such. I guess since losing George it didn't really feel like my safe place anymore.

"So, it's just you and your sister then?" Geoff asked curiously.

This boy is very inquisitive I thought. I've never had someone ask me so many questions or be interested to say the least.

"Well, it is now. I had a twin brother, George but he died just a couple of months ago during an air raid. You would've liked him." I say taking a deep breath to put my tears at bay.

"Oh god, I'm so sorry! I had no idea that must be awful. This bloody war! Its destroying so many families I can't wait for the day when it ends." Geoff replied bowing his head in despair.

It was only brief, but I could see the genuine pain in his eyes. I'd known him for five or ten minutes but there was something about him that intrigued me.

His kindness and his warmth drew me in and for the first time in a while I actually felt optimistic about the future.

Chapter 18
Naomi

"Well, I think that's enough for one day. I don't know about you but I'm starving," Grandma declared as she rubbed her belly.

"Hello? I'm back. Can you help me with the shopping please Naomi?" Mom shouted as she walked through the front doors struggling with shopping bags.

Mom's small Nissan Micra was overflowing with bags, Naomi was surprised how much she'd managed to fit in.

"Bloody hell Mom! Have you brought the whole shop?" Naomi laughed as she struggled with the last few bags and put them on the kitchen work top.

"I thought I'd stock up on a few items. Mainly tins really and we can freeze all the bread. That way I won't have to keep popping out and can focus on looking after your grandma." Mom replied as she tried to rearrange the freezer.

"Well, I'm always here mom. You know I don't mind looking after grandma. I'm putting a hold on the job search, just for a bit, until I can fully focus on it." Naomi said feeling guilty. However, she knew she'd have to start earning her own money at some point.

"I understand love. I'm sure your dad can help you with some money if you need. He's not short of a few bob or two." Mom laughed, as she put the kettle on.

6pm soon rolled round. Naomi had arranged to go to her dads for fajita night. It was something they used to do at home every two weeks, the four of them.

But tonight, it would be her dad, Stacey, and Naomi. It had taken a while, but Naomi felt ready to get to know Stacey, she was part of her father's life so to build a relationship back up with him she had to do the same with Stacey.

"You nervous love?" Mom asked as Naomi tied her shoelaces.

"A bit, kinda wish Clara was with me. Hopefully it'll go okay." Naomi replied trying to sound like she believed what she was saying.

"You'll be fine Naomi. Affairs are popular these days, stepparents are the rave!" Grandma said casually while knitting.

"Mom!" Mom cried, smirking.

"I'm only being honest love. You're happier without Neil, Neil's happier with Stacey. Bobs your uncle, Fannys your aunt."

"Very true Mom," mom replied as she rolled her eyes and smiled at Naomi.

The sound of a car horn made all three women jump.

"See you later!" Naomi said, after she gave her mom and grandma a kiss on the cheek goodbye.

Chapter 19

"Make yourself at home love, what would you like to drink? I've got gin, wine, coke, lemonade, or squash? Anything you want." Dad said as he hung Naomi's coat on the back of the front door.

"Squash is fine thank you." Naomi replied as she looked around the living room.

It was the first time she'd been to her dad's house. Clara had been and said how lovely it was, she was right.

Brown furnishings with plain white walls, covered in pictures of Clara and Naomi growing up.

"Naomi?" A faint female voice said as Naomi turned around to see who she assumed was Stacey.

Her long brown hair cascaded over her shoulders. She was wearing a baggy white jumper with leggings. She didn't look as young as Naomi imagined, she thought.

Naomi could see the nerves and worry in her expression. She strangely felt sorry for her. Like her grandma said, her mom and dad were both happy so there was no reason for Naomi to be angry. But part of her still was.

However, it was time to try she thought, no use in hanging on to anger. What good was that to anyone she thought?

"Hi! I love your jumper!" Naomi exclaimed trying to put her at ease.

"Oh, thanks! It's from Primark, only £8!" Stacey replied looking surprised but trying to act normal.

Dad was stood behind her holding Naomi's drink, looking just as shocked.

There were a few seconds of awkward silence but as soon as dad suggested they all sit at the table a relief rushed over Naomi. Maybe it wasn't going to be as bad after all.

As Stacey turned to walk to the table, Naomi noticed the small bump she was clearly trying to hide under her baggy jumper.

"So, when are you due?" Naomi asked trying to sound normal, but she couldn't help the slight squeak that came out as she spoke.

Dad and Stacey both looked at her with their eyes wide open, and a wave of worry ran over their face.

"Ummm we were going to tell you love. We just didn't want to spring it on you straight away and ideally tell you and Clara together, but I know that's difficult with her being at uni and er..." Dad said, rambling and fumbling with his hands.

"Dad its fine honestly. Your happy, I'm happy. You don't have to hide stuff from me to try and protect me. I'll admit I was very angry but it's time to accept things the way they are." Naomi said interrupting her dad to try and calm him down.

She saw the relief escape both him and Stacey. Their bodies relaxed and they were definitely smiling.

"I can't begin to tell you how much that means to me Naomi. You've honestly made my day!" Stacey beamed as she ran over to give her a hug.

The rest of the evening was spent laughing and reminiscing about when Naomi and Clara were little and getting up to mischief.

All three of them were relieved at how well the night had gone, all for their own separate reasons.

For Naomi it was nice to have a normal night filled with laughter and she was so glad that her relationship was back with her dad, she'd missed him.

Chapter 20

Wednesday, 3rd November. Naomi woke up to a frosty morning. She could feel the cold through her bedroom window as she got out of her warm bed and stretched.

As she walked onto the landing, she could smell fresh coffee and hear the theme tune of This Morning.

"What time do you call this lazy bones?" Mom asked buttering some toast.

"It's only 11 Mom, I didn't get back until late last night." Naomi replied stifling a yawn.

She had filled her mom in on the baby news, much to Naomi's surprise she was fine with it. She'd been expecting it apparently.

Dad was going to Facetime Clara tonight to tell her so that Naomi wouldn't have to keep it from her until she came home for Christmas.

"Could you take grandma's breakfast to her please love? I'm going to have a coffee and do my crossword," mom beamed.

Naomi walked in to find her grandma fixated on the television.

"Morning love. Blind me the things they talk about on this show! How to have an orgasm for 24 hours! I mean who would want that?" Grandma asked casually.

Naomi almost dropped the tea and toast; she was not expecting those words to come out of her grandmother's mouth!

"Well, they do call it entertainment!" Naomi laughed.

"Is your mother engrossed in her crossword yet?" Grandma asked with a mischievous look in her eyes.

"She is indeed. Coffee in hand, pen in the other," Naomi replied as she made herself comfy on the sofa.

"Right, I shall continue then…" Grandma declared as she propped her cushions.

Polly
Amsterdam December 1940

With only 5 days until Christmas day, it was time to decorate the tree. We only had a small artificial one this year. It was going to be our first one without George and quite frankly I could've done without it.

On the other hand, it didn't feel right to be celebrating Christmas. The world was suffering the loss of many soldiers and citizens, you could almost feel the sorrow in the atmosphere. Things just didn't sit right with me.

"It's not what we're used to kids but it'll do for this year." Mom said as she placed the last ball ball on the tree.

"Are we going to light a candle for George now?" Jane asked as she tugged at Moms pinafore.

I couldn't help but hold back tears at this point. The grief came in waves. One minute I was fine, the next I was crying myself to sleep, there was no in between.

Geoff had been incredible. He'd become my shoulder to cry on and my support mechanism. Even though he had never met George he tried so hard to keep his memory alive for me.

In the last couple of weeks, we'd become more than friends. I'll spare you the embarrassment of hearing about your grandmother's love life but what we had felt so special.

I'd wake up each morning with nervous belly ache and at times a grin from ear to ear. Geoff helped me manage my grief in a way that he often reminded me it's okay to go with my emotions and to never hold them in.

For a sixteen-year-old, he was so mature for his age. At times I felt like he was much older. My parents talked about George but not enough. I now realise it wasn't out of ignorance, but it was just too hard for them to even think about it.

"I'm going for a walk with Geoff, need anything from the shop?" I asked as I put on my wellies.

We'd had a bit of snow the past couple of days, but it had just started to freeze over with temperatures of -10 degrees. It was only going to get colder according to my father.

"Okay, be careful love, mind the ice and make sure you're back for five for tea." Mom shouted from the kitchen as she was preparing a stew.

"Can I come Polly?" Jane asked finishing her puzzle.

Nothing worse than when your eight-year-old little sister wants to tag along on a walk with your boyfriend I thought.

"It's too cold Jane, you'll just moan!" I said rolling my eyes.

"No, I won't! I love walking! Pleaseeeeee Polly! I'll tell mom and dad you're being mean," Jane declared as she stuck her tongue out at me.

She was so annoying. Mom and dad both thought the sun shone out of her arse, so there was no way I could say no to her.

"Sorry I had to bring her." I whispered to Geoff as we walked along the bridge.

"It's fine don't worry, I know what younger siblings are like," he smiled as he gave me a kiss on the cheek.

Jane was too busy collecting leaves to notice the sweet moment.

"Fancy getting a pick and mix Jane?" Geoff asked as he took her hand.

"Oh, yes please." Jane replied as she started skipping happily.

"Walk Jane, watch the ice!" I shouted as she scowled at me.

I rolled my eyes and Geoff gave me a reassuring look which made my stomach do multiple somersaults. I could feel my face burning up. I must've looked like a tomato.

Jane went into the shop to pick her sweets. Geoff wrapped his arm around me and pulled me closer to share our warmth. The cold mist was making my toes feel numb.

"Thank you for getting her sweets. She's not the easiest sister but at least we've still got each other." I said thinking about George.

"You'll get along better when she's older, she's just at her annoying age at the moment," Geoff replied calmly.

"I hope you're right. She seems to have been at the age from the moment she was born!" I laugh, rubbing my hands together to create some warmth.

"I got you a white chocolate mouse Geoff!" Jane said joyfully as she came out of the shop.

"Aww thank you. They're my favourite." Geoff replied genuinely.

I could see Jane blushing. Maybe it was the cold, or maybe she had a little crush on Geoff I thought.

"Did you get anything for me?" I asked feeling hopeful.

"No. You're getting fat, I thought I would do you a favour." Jane replied brazenly.

"Charming," I replied feeling my stomach. I'd only put a bit of weight on, but nothing major I thought.

"Just ignore her she doesn't know what she's talking about." Geoff whispered reassuringly as he put his arm around my waist.

We got back just in time for dinner. It was always hard saying bye to Geoff. Despite living next door, it felt like he was miles away when we parted.

We decided to keep our relationship a secret, that way our families couldn't interfere. As long as they thought we were friends we could continue going on our 'walks,' without receiving multiple questions from our parents.

"Did you have a nice walk girls?" Dad asked as we walked through the front door.

"Yeah, very cold though. Do you need any help with dinner mom?" I asked hanging up my coat.

"Should be okay love. It'll be another 15 minutes yet. Jane, can you lay the table please?" Mom asked rushing around the kitchen.

Jane huffed and puffed but she eventually put her pens down and went to help.

"Work have said we should be able to go home in February love, get back to some normality, eh?" Dad declared as he was doing his sudoku.

A rush of panic ran over me. I hadn't even considered going home. I'd been so distracted with Geoff that I hadn't even thought about it. What if we never saw each other again?

Hundreds of questions were racing through my mind, but I couldn't let dad witness my worry. I had to act normal.

"Oh cool, not long then." I replied, hoping he hadn't seen the dreaded look on my face.

I went to my bedroom with the hope that I could calm down. Writing always helps, so I picked up my diary to write todays entry.

As I was turning the pages, my stomach flipped to the point where I felt like I was going to be sick.

I was 8 weeks LATE.

My period was 8 weeks LATE.

I started sweating and my breathing became quicker and quicker.

How had I not noticed? How could I be so stupid to not realise?

I ran to my mirror to look at my stomach. Jane was right, I was getting fat.

I can't be I thought. I can't be pregnant...

"Polly, dinners ready!" Mom shouted making me jump a mile.

There was no point worrying now I thought, I have to act normal.

Chapter 21
Naomi

Naomi stared at her grandma in disbelief. The potential baby that she was on about couldn't possibly be her mom, so that meant there was another child, Naomi thought.

"Grandma, but…" Naomi said as she was interrupted.

"All in good time love. Now go and put the kettle on, I've built up quite the thirst." Grandma said leaning back in her chair.

Naomi couldn't believe what she'd just heard. She was expecting something big, but she certainly wasn't expecting that.

"You okay love? You look like you've seen a ghost," mom laughed as Naomi put the kettle on.

"Yeah, I'm fine just a bit tired that's all." Naomi replied hoping her mom wouldn't ask anymore questions.

It worked as she returned to her crossword.

Naomi had to tell Clara; this was something she couldn't take on herself. Surely her grandma wouldn't mind, she thought.

"Woah! What? Are you sure Naomi?" Clara asked after she'd been filled in via a phone call.

"Pretty sure Clara. I don't know when I'll find out the ending, but I don't know if I want to if I'm being honest. Imagine how upset mom will be." Naomi whispered down the phone, hoping neither women in the house would hear her.

"Well at least grandmas finally telling someone. I wonder if grandad knew. Bless her, she must've been so scared." Clara replied sounding concerned.

"Naomi, I'm going for a walk would you like to come? Grandmas going to have a nap." Mom shouted up the stairs.

"I've gotta go Clar, I'll text you later bye." Naomi hung up panicked by the sudden sound of her mom's voice.

Autumnal leaves covered the paths in the woods that Naomi and her mom walked through. It didn't seem as cold today as it had been but there was definitely a chill in the air.

The bare trees looked lonely as they waited for Summertime, but Naomi couldn't help but notice how pretty it was. It was the perfect post card picture for winter, she thought.

"When did grandma and grandad meet?" Naomi asked trying to put pieces together.

"Umm well grandma was 18 and grandad was 20 I believe. He had just got back from serving in the army. He was injured so couldn't fight for the last three years of the war. Your grandma always says it was a whirlwind romance. Why'd you ask?" Mom inquired.

"Oh, just wondered. I don't know why I've never really asked." Naomi replied feeling guilty.

"I'm sure grandma wouldn't mind. She's never really liked talking about life before grandad but she's open about pretty much anything else. You could write a book about their life!" Mom joked.

Naomi felt guilty knowing things that her mom didn't, she'd have to find out at some point she thought.

The rest of their walk involved them reminiscing and talking about Naomi's career options. They had this same talk every now and then, but Naomi still had no clue what she wanted to do.

Chapter 22

The last month had taken its toll on both Naomi and her mom. Grandma Polly had been in and out of hospital several times.

The medication that she was taking didn't seem to agree with her, she'd been fainting a lot and her confusion had gotten a lot worse.

But today, she was finally coming home. The right medication had been found and she was feeling like herself again, much to Naomi's relief.

"You look exhausted mom." Naomi said as she came down the stairs into the kitchen.

"I am love, once your grandma's home, I think I'll be able to rest more. Going back and forth to hospital is exhausting. Hopefully your grandma will rest more at home as well."

"Me and you both mom," Naomi replied yawning.

It was the 5th of December, Sunday. Mom was going to pick up grandma, while Naomi prepared a chicken roast dinner.

She'd never made one before, but she was willing to give it a go. It was her grandma's favourite, so something to make her feel better.

5 O'clock and mom and grandma were eventually home.

"Grandma!" Naomi ran over to her and gave her a gentle hug.

"Hello love. It's good to be home! Dinner smells delicious." Grandma said licking her lips.

She looked well, Naomi thought.

"Sorry we were so long; it took ages for them to sort the discharge papers and then we grabbed a quick coffee. Thank you for sorting dinner, we're very hungry." Mom said smiling.

As the three women tucked into their chicken dinner Naomi couldn't help but wonder how many times, they would be able to do this before the inevitable.

She couldn't help but notice her grandma looking frailer, she wished she could just freeze this moment for a while so she could appreciate it to its full potential.

"Well, it's definitely better than that awful hospital food!" Grandma declared, interrupting Naomi's thoughts.

"That's a relief. I've definitely got some practising to do." Naomi chuckled as she began clearing the plates.

"If I, were you, find a man who can cook. It's a bit better these days, women shouldn't be in the kitchen all the time. My mother slaved away while cooking and I don't really think my father ever appreciated it," grandma said taking a sip of her tonic water.

"Well, it's a good thing, things have changed eh mom. We've come a long way, still a bit to go through," mom winked looking over at Naomi as she began washing up.

9pm soon rolled round and Naomi and her grandma were watching repeats of Only Fools and Horses. It was one of Grandma Polly's favourite show, Naomi liked it too to be honest.

Mom had gone to bed about an hour ago, she was tired from all the running around over the last few days.

"I don't know about you Naomi, but I reckon I could stay up for another hour, shall I continue where I left off?" Grandma asked reclining in her armchair.

Naomi made herself comfortable eagerly waiting for what she would find out next.

Chapter 23
Polly – Amsterdam 1940

"Are you not hungry love?" Mom asked me as I pushed the food around with my fork. Eating was the last thing on my mind.

"I think she's trying to lose weight mommy; she's looking a bit podgy." Jane laughed

"Jane ………! Don't be so rude and apologise to your sister immediately!" My father shouted across the table, making me jump.

It was the first time I had seen him angry. He had told us off before, but never shouted that loud. It wouldn't surprise me if the neighbours came round to check if everything was ok.

Jane immediately began to cry and left the table running to her bedroom.

Just as my mother got up to go after her my father put out his hand to stop her.

"Leave her she needs to learn some manners and not act so spoilt all the time." My father declared calmly.

This was a first. Usually, Jane always got her way but maybe it was time she learnt a lesson I thought.

"And you're not getting fat Polly, you're perfect just the way you are." My father said smiling at me as he finished his food.

His comment made me feel better, but I couldn't help but feel guilty at the same time. If I am pregnant the shame, I would bring on the family would be unforgivable, I thought to myself.

Eventually, I managed to eat some food, but I felt exhausted so decided to get an early night.

I woke up early the next morning and as soon as I opened my eyes my stomach churned, and I ran to the bathroom, immediately being sick.

My head was spinning, and I didn't even have the strength to move my head from the toilet.

"Polly?" I heard my mother outside the bathroom.

Bugger, how would I explain this I thought.

"Can I come in?" Mother asked me sounding concerned.

She must know, she must be suspicious I thought.

"Yes," I replied feeling weak.

"Oh, love you must have a stomach bug, maybe that's why you couldn't eat much last night." My mother said kneeling down beside me and stroking my head.

Relief ran over me, maybe she was right, maybe it was just a stomach bug, I thought. But deep down I knew.

A month past and I was getting bigger. I still managed to hide it with baggy jumpers and by just staying in my room to read. But sooner or later I knew I would have to confess.

I missed Geoff terribly. It was like my heart had been ripped out and stomped on as well as horrendous morning sickness.

Geoff had called round several times, but my mother just told him I had stomach flu which is what she believed at the time.

I eventually plucked up the courage to leave my room.

"Feeling better love?" My mother asked as she folded the ironing, still not noticing my tummy luckily.

"A little bit, I'm going to go for a walk if that's ok. I need some fresh air." I said feeling claustrophobic.

"Can I come?" Jane whined before catching my serious glare.

"No." I snapped without thinking.

Jane just stared at me looking shocked as if she was going to burst into tears any second.

"Just let Polly go on her own Jane. We can do some colouring once I've finished this." Mom said giving me a reassuring look.

I grabbed my coat, hat, and scarf and took a deep breath. I needed to tell Geoff; it was time.

Chapter 24
Naomi
2010

"Right time for bed for me," grandma said mid yawn.

"Ah grandma, you always leave it on a cliff hanger! I swear you do it on purpose," Naomi laughed.

"Trust me its better in stages my dear, and we both need our beauty sleep." Grandma smiled as she steadily got out of her armchair.

Naomi didn't know whether to take that offensively or not, but she could definitely do with a good night's sleep.

The next morning swiftly arrived which marked five days until Clara would be home for Christmas. Naomi couldn't wait.

"Have you heard about Christmas?" Clara asked Naomi over the phone.

"What? Oh, please tell me you're still coming!" Naomi asked dreading the answer.

"Of course, I am! Wouldn't miss it for the world. But mom said she was thinking of asking dad and Stacey over too!" Clara replied.

"What? No way. That surprises me, do you know why?" Naomi asked feeling confused and upset their mom hadn't mentioned it to her.

"Well, apparently Stacey is really anxious about the baby and dads all stressed. But imagine how awkward it's going to be." Clara said trying not to laugh.

"Well, if mom offered hopefully, it won't be. Will be nice to have a family Christmas, well sort of for grandma's sake anyway." Naomi replied, feeling grown up for once.

"Bloody hell, what's happened to you being the mature one?" Clara laughed.

"I'm surprised myself to be honest," Naomi laughed.

"Proud of you sis. Well, I better go get these last two assignments completed," Clara moaned down the phone.

"Naomi! Breakfast is ready." Mom shouted up the stairs.

Naomi walked down to the smell of soda bread, sausage, eggs, and bacon.

"Smells delicious, what's the occasion?" Naomi asked, her mouth salivating.

"Well, it was on grandma's orders, and we haven't had one in a while, so I thought why not?" Mom replied as she poured some orange juice into three separate glasses.

Grandma was sat in the lounge fixated with her knitting, with Holly and Phil on in the background.

Just as the three women tucked into their breakfast moms phone started ringing.

"It's always the way isn't it!" Mom moaned mid chew, as she walked into the kitchen to take the call.

"I wonder if it's her new lover?" Grandma casually suggested to Naomi.

"What? Moms seeing someone? She hasn't said anything." Naomi replied feeling surprised.

"Oh, I'm just guessing love, but she's been tapping away a lot on that phone and smiling." Grandma said eyes still fixated on her English breakfast.

It was no surprise to Naomi that her mom would meet somebody eventually, she was gorgeous, and had the best personality.

"Aw your Auntie Karen has booked us in for a spa afternoon at the Malvern Spa, how lovely is that?" Mom said coming into the room smiling.

Naomi and her grandma both had a little smile to each other.

Auntie Karen wasn't related but she was Naomi's moms' best friend since school so to Clara and Naomi she had always been 'Auntie Karen.'

Naomi had a sneaky suspicion it may be this new man her grandma had suggested but either way it was good to see the happy glow on her face again.

2pm quickly came round and mom was off for her spa afternoon.

Naomi had received yet again another job rejection email. She'd been applying for different types of industries and hoping but nothing had worked out so far.

"What's the glum face for love?" Grandma asked Naomi who had noticed her shoulders drop.

"Just another rejection email. Oh well, someone's gotta want me," Naomi replied trying to make light of the situation.

"Want me to carry on with my story? I'm not sure it'll cheer you up though," grandma said looking concerned.

"I would love to," Naomi replied feeling a genuine relief.

Chapter 25
Polly
Amsterdam 1941

The snap of the cold air hit me as soon as I stepped out of our building. I don't know whether it was the nerves getting the better of me or the temperature had really dropped.

Christmas had come and gone. I don't even think I made it out of bed on the day itself.

So, 1941, a new year and I was 99% sure I was pregnant. The fear of telling my parents was too much to even think about. So, I decided I needed to tell Geoff.

My trembling hand unlocked the door and despite the freezing temperatures my hands were clammy with sweat. I felt like any moment my heart was going to jump out of my chest.

Mrs Janson opened the door with the usual welcoming smile on her face.

"Hello love, are you feeling better?" She asked me as her eyes immediately went towards my stomach.

I still don't know whether I was being paranoid but I'm pretty sure she knew. Nevertheless, she carried on smiling and called for Geoff.

Geoff came rushing out and looked at me as if he hadn't seen me in years.

Butterflies soon started flying around my stomach and I couldn't help but feel relief the moment I laid eyes on him.

"Polly!" He shouted running over to me to give me the warmest of hugs.

We began walking, trying to avoid the black ice. My nerves got the better of me, so I just asked questions about what he'd been doing.

"I can't believe you missed Christmas! You must've felt bad!" Geoff said showing his concern.

"I know. I was kind of dreading it anyway. It was never going to be the same without George." I replied feeling a lump at the back of my throat.

Geoff took my hand and squeezed it tight. He didn't say anything, but I knew his love for me was still there and he would look after me.

We went to our spot. It had become our go to space when Jane wasn't with us.

It was a tunnel that in the Summer Geoff said flowers were planted around it to create a symbol of hope and peace. The frost had killed the flowers, but we had made a den in there to make it cosy and used candles which provided warmth.

Geoff had to duck to walk in, but I was short enough not to. We sat side by side on the blankets as Geoff lit the candles.

The streets were quiet, it was getting late. Geoff put his hand on my leg and kissed my cheek softly.

"I've missed you," Geoff whispered gently in my ear.

"Your birthday in a couple of weeks, 17. I can't wait to be 17," I sighed trying to avoid my problems.

"What's the rush? We've got our whole lives ahead of us, well after this bloody war." Geoff sighed bowing his head.

"Yes, I suppose. It's just… oh I don't know. I'm just not used to being out it feels weird." I laughed nervously.

Geoff looked at me with a complexed expression on his face. I couldn't quite work out what he was thinking.

"You don't seem yourself. I mean I know you've been poorly, but you look worried. What's wrong?" Geoff asked me looking concerned.

He gently put his arm around me, his way of reassuring me I thought.

The lump in the back of my throat felt like it was getting bigger. I felt physically sick but knew I had to tell him. It was like ripping off a plaster I told myself, a big one.

"I think… I think I might be pregnant," as those words trickled out of my mouth, I felt a sense of relief.

But at the same time, I was scared. It was the first time I had spoken those words. For the last couple of months, they had just been stuck in my head. It was like I was setting them free.

Geoff's arm relaxed and he slowly removed it from around my shoulders.

Silence filled the air. It was the first time either of us had been lost for words.

"You think, or, you're sure?" Geoff asked me without removing his eyes from the ground.

"Well, I'm not one hundred percent sure but, I've missed two periods now and…" I replied as I lifted my jumper to show a small but noticeable bump.

"So, pretty certain," Geoff said looking at my stomach with shock and sadness in his eyes.

It was at this point; I couldn't bury my emotions any longer.

A stream of tears ran down my cheeks and I became inconsolable.

Geoff pulled me into his chest and held me until I couldn't cry any longer.

"It's going to be okay. We'll get married and we'll become a family. I love you; this doesn't change that. I'm just in shock that's all," Geoff said trying to reassure me.

"Married?" I said feeling like a deer caught in headlights.

"Yes, like you said we're almost 17, we're practically adults, we'll just need our parents' permission," Geoff said so calmly as if he'd been practising.

"You don't understand, my father is going to want to kill me and then he'll come after you." I said panicking, trying to catch my breath.

"Why? We're in love, aren't we? I know I am, I'm sure he'll come round if I show him how much I care about you and prove to him I'll look after you and our baby." Geoff declared looking at me with his deep blue eyes.

"Of course, I do! I just think it'll be a shock. I'm still trying to come to terms with it myself." I said feeling guilty.

"I know you are, but I will look after you I promise, and if that means proving myself to your family then I will do everything I can." Geoff replied sounding confident.

Chapter 26
Naomi 2010

"You can stop if it's getting too much grandma," Naomi said noticing the emotional strain it was having on her grandma, just from the look on her face.

Naomi felt emotional herself. She couldn't even begin to imagine how scared her grandma would have felt, especially with a war going on and not long after losing her twin brother George.

"I think I'm just tired love. I might go and have a lie down. Fancy making a start on dinner?" Grandma asked Naomi, as she made her way to her bedroom.

"Yeah sure, have a good rest," Naomi said feeling guilty that her grandma was having to relive her past again.

Just as Naomi was looking in the fridge to decide what to cook there was a gentle knock at the front door.

Naomi opened it to find an older looking man holding a bunch of beautiful flowers.

"Hello" Naomi said looking confused as she didn't recognise the man.

"Hello, sorry to disturb you, I hope I haven't come at a bad time. I'm Doctor Fabien, I looked after your grandmother when she first came into hospital, I think we met briefly." He said, nervously.

"Oh of course sorry, I recognise you now you've said. I'm afraid my grandma is having a nap and my mom's out at the moment. Is there anything I can help with?" Naomi asked wondering why the doctor was visiting.

"Oh, no not to worry, I just wanted to pass on these flowers to your grandmother. They're from myself and some of the nurses on the ward. Your grandmother is a real character and we just wanted to say thank you for making our shifts a little easier," Doctor Fabian replied smiling.

Fabian passed the colourful flowers to Naomi, who took them with a warm smile on her face.

"Wow. They're lovely. Thank you so much, I'm sure they will really brighten my grandma's day." Naomi replied feeling very grateful.

Fabian smiled and walked away to his car which was parked at the end of the drive.

"Who is it, Naomi?" Grandma shouted from the front room.

"I thought you were having a sleep grandma!" Naomi cried as she walked in the living room, holding the flowers.

"Wow. They're beautiful. Who is he then? You never told me you had an admirer!" Grandma looked inquisitively at Naomi.

"It's not me whose got the admirer. Some of the hospital staff have bought them for you. Doctor Fabian just dropped them round. Isn't that nice?" Naomi said as she began to arrange them in a vase.

"Oh, how lovely! Now your mother will believe me, about being their favourite patient!" Grandma said feeling happy and content.

7 O'clock soon came round, and just as grandma was stirring from her nap in the armchair, mom returned with rosy, red cheeks.

"Had a nice day mom? I thought you would be back later." Naomi said as she put her magazine back on the coffee table.

"The best. We had a lovely facial, and the spa is to die for," mom exclaimed with a spring in her step.

"Very nice, I've not long put a quiche in the oven for tea if you want any?" Naomi suggested as she surfed through the television channels.

"I'm okay thanks love, we had a big lunch. But if you pop it in the fridge after I'll have some for lunch tomorrow." Mom replied.

Naomi explained the kind gesture of flowers to her mom and then she went to prepare the tea for her and her grandma.

"This is lovely, Naomi, did you make it yourself?" Grandma asked as she tucked in.

"Of course not! It's just a shop bought one. I'm good but I'm not that good" Naomi laughed as she got herself comfortable in front of the television.

It was officially a week until Christmas and Naomi couldn't wait to see Clara, who was also bringing her boyfriend, Josh.

Their train was due to arrive at Worcester Foregate Street tomorrow at 2pm, so their mom was picking her and Josh up.

"I bet you can't wait to see Clara. It'll be nice to hear all about Liverpool and suss out that boyfriend of hers," grandma said, placing her tray on the coffee table.

"I can't! It's gone quite quick actually and he seems lovely." Naomi replied feeling excited.

"I'm sure you've been keeping her up to date with things," grandma declared.

Naomi didn't know what to say. She had been filling Clara in but not to betray their grandma, purely so that she had someone else to talk to about it.

"Don't look so worried love. I thought you would tell young Clara anyway. I would've told you both is she wasn't at university. I'm sure you'll tell your mother when the times right," grandma said reassuringly.

Naomi felt relieved, but she wasn't sure what her grandma meant by when the times right. Did she mean when she got too poorly? Naomi didn't want to think about it but told herself she would cross that bridge when she came to it.

....

Sunday lunch time soon arrived, and Naomi couldn't wait to be reunited with her twin. They spoke every day on the phone, but it just wasn't the same.

127

"I've got to pop to the shops to get some bread and milk on the way to the train station if that's okay love?" Mom asked Naomi.

They'd just had a late breakfast so were watching some Sunday television. The weather outside was dull and gloomy, it was winter after all, Naomi thought.

"Yeah sure, are we still getting a takeaway tonight?" Naomi asked. She hadn't had a takeaway in months she thought.

In the build up to Christmas routine went out the window and because mom was so busy with present prep and dad was busy at work, the four of them made the most of the two-week relaxation.

"I think so. I can't be bothered to cook if I'm being honest. Good of your dad and Stacey to come and keep grandma company while we go and pick up the love birds," mom laughed, she was happy to see Clara so happy.

Dad had apparently offered to sit with grandma so that he could see Clara when she got back. He had said it was the least he could do as been as mom was doing Christmas lunch for everyone.

The drive to Foregate Street didn't take them long and was only a short walk from their house. But Clara and Josh were staying for two weeks so mom said they would have too much to carry.

"Gosh, you can tell it's almost Christmas with this traffic," mom sighed as she put the gear stick into neutral while they sat at a standstill.

"Clara said they're going to grab a coffee while they wait. Do you want one?" Naomi asked her mom as she read the text from Clara.

"Oh okay, I'll have an Americano please, tell her I'll pay for them. I can't believe a 10-minute journey has already taken half an hour, we left early as well." Mom moaned banging the wheel with her hands.

"Can't believe it's Christmas in a few days. It's gone surprisingly quick." Naomi said, trying to stop the thought that was entering her mind. But she couldn't help it, realistically it would be her grandmas last Christmas despite her doing so well.

"Tell me about it. I'm so glad I'm just doing money this year. It's so much easier and less stressful." Mom said interrupting Naomi's thoughts.

Finally, after 45 minutes Mom parked up on the high street and went into Costa to help Clara and Josh with their luggage.

Naomi waited outside the car so she could open the boot for all the luggage.

"Naomi!" Clara shouted running towards the car.

The twins gave each other the warmest of hugs and suddenly everything felt like it was going to be okay.

"Lovely to see you again Josh!" Naomi said as she leant in to give him a hug.

"Likewise! Four weeks of no assignments and my first English Christmas. I can not wait!" Josh squealed in his strong Australian accent as he got in the car.

Naomi could just tell from the atmosphere in the car it was going to be a good Christmas, one to remember she thought.

Chapter 27
Clara

It was so good to be home. Don't get me wrong Liverpool was great and I'm really making the most of the uni life but there was nothing more comforting than home sweet home.

From the moment I found out about Grandma Polly being ill, it had been the one constant thing on my mind. I've lost count the number of times I'd cried to Josh before going to sleep, but I've tried my best to hide it in from Naomi.

I've always been the strongest twin, Naomi would agree. So, I've always been the shoulder to cry on or the one to act brave, even if inside a river was on the verge of flooding.

Throughout the divorce of my parents, Naomi was angry, sad, and so disappointed in our dad, and I was all of those emotions too. But I had to look at it realistically and try and prevent Naomi from making the biggest mistake of her life which would be completely cutting out our dad.

He was in the wrong fully, but at the same time our mom hadn't been happy in a while and I could see that, which is why I needed to be strong for her too.

But I knew at the end of day she would be the one to come out of it happy, even if it took a while, and I could see that now.

From the moment our eyes met in Costa, the glow on her face was something special. Her rosy cheeks and the happy glint she had in her eye was something I hadn't seen in years, and a weight definitely lifted off my shoulders.

"I thought we'd have a Chinese or Indian for tea if that's alright with you love?" Mom suggested as she pulled into the drive.

"Sure, Josh has found a love for sweet and sour chicken balls lately," I laughed, as I got out of the car.

"They are the best, probably not great for you, but they still provide a fleeting moment of bliss." Josh added lipping his lips.

"You can't beat Singapore noodles Josh, although I am partial to a chicken ball or two," mom smiled as dad opened the door to help us with our stuff.

"There she is, the brain of the family," dad stated as he walked up to me to give me one of his bear hugs.

"Charming," Naomi huffed, lifting my study bag.

I laughed but gave Naomi a sympathised look. She didn't take it seriously though, she just smiled.

"Hi Stacey, you're looking well," I said walking into the kitchen to see Stacey making tea for everyone. Her bump was looking big, and she looked well despite the tiredness I could see under her eyes.

I'd spoken to Stacey a lot while being at uni. Whenever I rang to speak to dad, she always answered the phone and took a real interest in me asking about how I was getting on and checking in, to see how I was coping about grandma.

I hadn't put a brave face on for her. I was open and honest but not because I felt I couldn't with Naomi but because it didn't directly affect Stacey, so I found it easier.

"Thank you, Clara, so lovely to see you!" Stacey replied which a beaming smile.

It was so nice to see my dad and Stacey happy and so right for each other. Yeah, it was rubbish at the time, but it seemed to have worked out for the better I thought.

Both parents affected but both doing so well and closer than ever, it was so nice to see.

"Young Clara?" Grandma called me from the living room, I couldn't wait to see her.

"Grandma! Ahhh, you look so well, did you wear your favourite blouse for me?" I asked grinning from ear to ear, as I knelt down to give her a long-awaited hug.

The fuchsia pink blouse she was wearing really brought out her light blue eyes. She did look well, better than I was expected if I'm being honest, I thought.

"Of course, I did. Come on then tell me all about Liverpool and that handsome boyfriend of yours," Grandma said with a smirk as she squeezed my hand warmly.

Chapter 28
Naomi

It was so good to have Clara home, Naomi thought. It was like she'd never left.

"How are you getting on with the job applications Naomi?" Stacey asked as they sat down in the kitchen with tea and biscuits. Clara was filling their grandma in on her university antics and all things law.

"Not very well unfortunately. Just one rejection email after another. I was going to ask dad if he could have a look at my CV, maybe help me jazz it up a bit." Naomi laughed, but deep down he was feeling hurt and disappointed.

"Well, as it happens Stacey was thinking about going on maternity leave early some time next month. So, do you fancy being my secretary working towards an apprenticeship in law? I know it's not what you've really thought about, but it'll be good money for a bit." Dad suggested cutting a Victoria sponge for everyone.

Naomi hadn't really considered law as an option. She'd always known it was Clara's dream, but nothing really stood out to her career wise. But she desperately wanted to earn some money.

"Sounds good dad, I think it'll do me good to start something. You never know I might actually enjoy it," Naomi replied feeling optimistic.

The rest of the afternoon was spent laughing and trying to embarrass Clara as much as possible in front of Josh.

Clara was being a good sport just taking it on the chin like a true trooper.

"I think I might go and have a nanna nap." Grandma declared as she edged herself forward to shuffle off her armchair.

"I don't blame you Ms Madden, I feel exhausted myself all this laughing and winding up Clara, it's a lot to carry," Josh said amusingly.

They were a match made in heaven Naomi thought to herself.

"Please call me Polly, Josh. You've got my approval." Grandma smiled and tapped him on the shoulder as she made her way to her bedroom.

Naomi and Clara both gave Josh a look as if to say, you've done well.

As soon as they caught each other doing it they both burst into a fit of laughter.

Chapter 29
Naomi

Monday soon came round. Mom was doing a day shift at work, while Naomi and Clara had a proper catch up.

Josh had gone to do some Christmas shopping, once Clara had given him directions into town. She'd offered to go with him, but Josh had said it would ruin her present, so she was more than happy to stay in the warm.

"It was nice to have dad and Stacey here yesterday, wasn't it? I thought Stacey did well, considering she must've been so nervous and mom of course," Clara said to Naomi as the girls made a festive hot chocolate.

"Yeah definitely, felt like the good old times and grandma seemed to enjoy it apart from feeling tired." Naomi replied, feeling worn out herself. It must've been the excitement she thought.

"Oooo I'll have one of those if you don't mind?" Grandma said sneaking up behind Naomi and Clara and eyeing up the calorific hot chocolate.

"Coming right up your highness," Clara replied smiling.

Grandma looked well, Naomi thought. She'd had a long lie in but who wouldn't on a cold and gloomy day like today.

"Now I was thinking…" Grandma said before Naomi interrupted.

"Be careful that's dangerous," Naomi said jokingly.

Grandma looked at her trying to suppress a laugh but carried on, nevertheless.

"As been as your mother is at work and young Josh is out shopping, could I have some time with the two of you? I want to share my last little bit with you both together if that's alright?" Grandma asked looking at Clara and Naomi intently.

Naomi and Clara both looked at each other, they were nervous but at the same time curious.

"Of course, grandma, we'd be honoured," Naomi replied looking reassuringly at Clara.

Chapter 31
Polly
Amsterdam January 1941

The walk back with Geoff was weird. It was quiet. Something I wasn't used to with him.

He continued to reassure me, but his words were just getting lost in the dreaded thought of having to tell my mother and father. I didn't know whether I should tell my mother first or both together.

I came to the conclusion that it would be easier to tell them together because at least that way I didn't have to do it twice.

"Come and get me if you need. Are you sure you don't want me to come with you?" Geoff asked me, with concern in his eyes.

"No, I'll be ok. I need to do this on my own." I said sounding firm but not meaning to.

Geoff embraced me and it felt like he wasn't going to let me go until he relaxed his arms and gave me a soft kiss on my forehead.

"I love you." He said looking into my eyes deeply.

"I love you too," I replied trying to relax my tense posture.

"Did you have a nice walk love? You've been a while; dinner is almost ready." My mother said to me as I walked in, and she was laying the table.

I knew she had noticed the white complexion on my face, from the moment she looked at me. The worry and anxiousness were plastered on my face, and I felt like I would break any moment.

"Your face love. What's the matter, has somebody hurt you? Do you feel poorly again? Want me to get you a bowl?" My mother bombarded questions at me one after another.

"I need, I need to, to talk to you and dad." I said, the words struggling to escape my mouth.

"Ok love. You're scaring me. I'll go and get your father, Jane go to your room please, start reading your new book." My mother said as she went to get my father from his study.

Jane looked at me and then started walking to her room without saying anything. She was speechless for a change.

I sat down at the dining table and tried to calm my thoughts. I needed to think realistically. I thought to myself that my mother and father wouldn't be angry with me about the pregnancy itself but the fact I wasn't married and hadn't even told them about Geoff.

They would be mad that I had lied to them and gone behind their back. My father hated liars and most of all he hated his children lying to him.

All these thoughts were racing through my mind. But it was time to own up to my mistakes and face them, it was time to tell the truth.

"What's wrong Polly. Your mother said you wanted to speak to us. She is ever so worried." My father said as they both joined me at the table.

My mother looked as worried as me. Her face was white, and her eyes looked sad.

"I know you're going to be mad with me and angry. But please remember that I'm sorry and I really need you to support me and look after me," I said calmly surprising myself that I had managed to sound strong.

My parents didn't say anything, they just looked at me with an expression which prompted me to continue.

"I'm pregnant." I said, without thinking about it. As soon as the words were set free, I felt a moment of relief until I saw the look on my parent's face. A look I will never forget.

My father looked disappointed and sad at the same time. Slowly, he got out of his chair and returned to his study.

My mother just looked at me in shock. I didn't know what she was going to say but I needed her to say something, anything.

But slowly she got up off her seat walked over to me calmly and slapped me across the face. She then proceeded to carry on cooking.

The right side of my face was burning from her force, my anger, and my sadness. Words failed me and I made my way to my bedroom.

A short while later, Jane came into my room. She looked at me, with sadness in her eyes. I didn't have the energy or capability to tell ger to go away.

She gently walked towards me and put her small hands on my tummy. She looked deep into my eyes and proceeded to give me the warmest of hugs.

"It's going to be ok Polly. I'll look after you." Jane whispered as her head rested on my chest, and with that I burst into tears.

The only sound you could hear as we sat down to eat dinner, was the cutlery moving around our plates.

My father hadn't made eye contact with me since and my mother just glared at me.

Jane said she wasn't hungry so continued to play with her toys, which neither of my parents seemed bothered about.

"Geoff has proposed, and we're going to get married and become a family," I said quickly, trying to break the tension.

"Well, you should have got married before any of this had of happened if that's the case. After everything this family has been through, how could you be so stupid Polly? Did it every cross your mind the shame you would bring on this family?

"Geoff lives here in Amsterdam. You live in London. The moment we get home and believe you me that will be in the next few weeks. Our family will be shamed and excluded from society. Did any of this cross your mind?" My mother said in a raised voice while glaring at me the entire time.

My father still hadn't looked at me, his eyes were just fixated on the table.

Of course, I knew I had been stupid, I hadn't been thinking and therefore reckless. But deep down I thought my parents would be more supportive at least and not look at me like a rat they'd come across on the street.

"You'll get married. You'll have the baby, and none of this will be spoken about again. Do you understand?" My father said sternly, his glare forced upon me.

I didn't say anything. There was no room for negotiation or discussion, what my father said is what will happen, I thought to myself.

My mother huffed, rolled her eyes, and began clearing up the dishes.

Geoff met me outside at 9pm. I hadn't spoken to my parents since dinner and didn't plan to for the rest of the evening.

"It's done. My parents pretty much hate me but in my father's words we get married, we have the baby and never utter a word of it again." I said, standing in the freezing cold.

Geoff just looked at me. A look I hadn't seen before, he looked scared, worried, and ashamed.

"I have to leave. I'll be back but I don't know when, my family and I we have to go. We must hide." Geoff said, avoiding my eyeline.

Chapter 32
Polly
Amsterdam

I stood there frozen to the spot, unable to fathom what had just been said.

"What? What do you mean you have to go?" I asked Geoff, severely confused.

"There are rumours," Geoff muttered.

"Rumours? What rumours? You're not making any sense Geoff." I said, feeling frustrated and annoyed.

"I've never told you before, not because I'm ashamed or that it was any sort of secret but I'm Jewish." Geoff replied, his head tilted towards the ground.

"I don't understand. What has that got to do with anything. Why does it mean you need to leave?" I said feeling even more confused.

"My father has heard these awful stories. At first, we thought it was fake, because how could a human being be so awful. But then we've heard more things, worse things and we can't just ignore it.

"We don't fit in with the Nazi ideology, I don't know why, and I don't know how but if we want to live, we have to run. But just me. I'm not putting you or our baby at risk, under any circumstances. If I, can we will come back and I'll come to London with you, I promise." Geoff sobbed as he put his hands on my shoulders.

"But you can't just go I need you. I'll speak to my parents and see if we can leave earlier, and you can come with us. I just don't understand. Why is this happening?" I cried, unable to control my emotions any longer.

"I can't leave my family Pol. I need to be with them. We're leaving at noon tomorrow, I'll come and say goodbye, and I'll explain to your parents. I am so so sorry, I never thought this would happen. But my mother is so worried I need to protect her and my sister, I have no choice." Geoff said looking exhausted and emotionally drained.

I wanted to scream, shout, and tell him he did have a choice. He could choose me and our baby, but that wasn't who I was. That wasn't me. If I was in his position, I really wouldn't know what I would do.

I would want to protect my family as much as possible. But I wasn't in his position, and I couldn't even begin to imagine the turmoil he was going through, I could just see the strain on his face.

"I'm sorry I can't be certain about when I'll be back, but if you're not here I'll come and find you. I won't stop until I find you." Geoff declared trying to reassure me, but it was just making me sadder.

"This can't be how we end. I hate war." I cried, feeling deflated.

"Me too. This isn't how we end. I promise. I love you." Geoff said and he leaned in to give me a passionate kiss which I wish could have lasted forever.

"I love you," I whispered trying to take every last second of him in.

145

"I will call in at 9am in the morning to see you and talk to your parents, I promise." Geoff said softly and with that he was gone. I stood there shaking in the cold, hoping I was stuck in some awful nightmare.

But I wasn't. This was real and there was nothing I could do about it.

Chapter 33
Polly

The next morning arrived, or rather hit me like a brick. I'd only slept for around two hours. I'd been tossing and turning throughout the night trying to come up with a solution, but I couldn't. I felt useless.

I hadn't spoken to my parents when I'd come back in. I didn't even know what to say, because I couldn't properly process it myself.

I went into the kitchen to find tea and toast on the table.

"You need to keep your strength up. You're eating for two now." My mother said sternly, but I could tell she still cared about me which was somewhat of a relief.

"Thank you," I responded feeling shaky and worried.

It was thirty minutes before Geoff would be there saying his final goodbyes and explaining what was happening to my parents.

I wanted to do it myself, to take the added pressure of him, but I couldn't even find the words or the strength.

9am arrived and went. Geoff hadn't come. He wouldn't have left without saying goodbye I thought. But what if it was too hard for him or they had to leave earlier.

What if that was the last time, I was going to see him? No. It couldn't be, it wouldn't be, it can't be I thought.

"Love. Calm down. Breath. Slow deep breaths. In, out, in out." My mother started telling me as she knelt down to the side of me.

I hadn't even noticed my breathing had become erratic. I couldn't control it, but slowly I did. Eventually my breathing became steady, and my thoughts settled.

"There we go. That's better. Why don't you go and get Geoff to come round, and we can have a proper conversation? I'll make some tea." My mother suggested, as if she had come to terms with the news a little bit more.

She was right I thought, I'll go round there. He wouldn't have just gone.

I approached his front door with trepidation. His family was already going through so much and I really didn't want to make it harder for them, but I needed to see him. There were things I needed to say.

As I went to knock the door, I put very little pressure on it with my knuckles, but I caused it to be ajar. It was open and looked like the lock had been broken.

My stomach sank.

I walked in cautiously to see their home destroyed. Tables were turned, chairs were upside down and belongings were thrown everywhere, with no care.

I was in shock; I was confused and at the same time frightened. But in the back of my mind, I knew.

Geoff was right. The rumours were true. But at the same time, I wasn't sure, maybe they had just had to leave earlier than they had planned.

Several different scenarios crossed my mind and I instantly walked towards his bedroom, to see if I could work out what had happened.

There I saw it, a letter addressed to me. A sign. But what it would reveal scared me.

I opened it, my fingers trembling and my heart pounding. The writing was rushed as if he hadn't had long to write it.

Dearest Polly,

You're reading this because we ran out of time. We underestimated the situation and had no choice but to listen to orders. I'll never understand why this has had to happen, and I'll never be able to fully explain the sickening feeling that I have.

My biggest regret is not being able to be with you. I don't know if or when I'll see you again, but I so hope I do. I don't really know what to expect or how long we will be kept.

I so hope your parents understand and allow you to keep and look after our baby, because trust me when I say that will keep me going and I will never forget you. Until we meet again.

All my love forever and always
Geoff
xxxx

Chapter 34
Naomi

Grandma Polly handed the letter to Naomi and Clara. It was old and worn but the ink stain was still readable.

Both girls looked at it with sadness in their eyes. They couldn't believe what they had just heard and felt so sad to know their grandma had been through all of that.

"I'm so sorry grandma," Clara cried noticing the strain it had put on her and the torment it must have caused all these years.

"Me too. It's so awful. What happened after, did you ever see each other again?" Naomi asked, she felt bad, but she wanted to know. The baby couldn't be their mother.

"I explained what had happened to my parents. My father said that I would have the baby in Amsterdam and that he would arrange for it to be put up for adoption. My mother tried to reason with him, but I had no choice.

"I never saw Geoff again. When we found out about the concentration camps that's what I assumed had happened. I didn't know for certain but deep down I did. I grieved twice. Once for our son and once for him." Grandma responded struggling to get her words out because of the emotion.

"Don't continue if it's too much grandma, we understand." Clara said, she didn't but she didn't want to put her grandma through anymore upset.
Nevertheless, their grandmother continued, she wanted to get everything out in the open.

"I gave birth to George six months later. I was dreading the birth because I knew the moment it had happened; I would have to say goodbye.

"Geoff and I had had a conversation previously before I was pregnant about baby names, and we'd both agreed if we had a boy, he would be named George, after my brother. So that was a promise I could keep.

"He was gorgeous. I'm biased but he really was. I had half an hour with him, half an hour too short, but I made the very most of it. I pleaded and begged my father to let me keep him, but I had no choice, my father wouldn't even look me in the eye. I never looked at him the same way again.

"As soon as George was taken, we had to make our way back to London. Our family broke the moment my brother died, but it broke again for good this time. I had the best relationship with Jane that we had ever had, and my mother and I were close because she had tried but my father and I never had a good relationship after. I never forgave him.

"I know it was different in those days, but I would do anything for Katherine and you girls, anything. I met your grandfather two years later in Malvern when I was on a nursing placement.

"We started off as friends and I told him everything. He made no judgement and just listened. It wasn't long after that we fell in love, it was a different kind of love but one that I wouldn't change for the world.

"He helped me look for George, but we just kept going down dead ends and I felt like I was going down a downwards spiral, and I needed to be strong for your mother, so I stopped.

"I told your grandfather I didn't want to speak about it again. He tried to change my mind, but he understood and never pressured me. He really was one of a kind.

"I've never told your mother because I just haven't been able to find the words. I know it's a lot to ask but do you think you could both tell her together when I'm gone.

"I feel my mind is not as strong as it once was, and I know I'm deteriorating but I want to spend the rest of my time living in the moment and not the past. I know it's a lot to ask." Grandma said feeling guilty but at the same time relieved.

Naomi and Clara both looked at each other not knowing what to say but they sympathised with their grandmother.

"Of course, we will respect your wishes grandma. I'm sure mom will understand." Naomi said, hoping what she'd said was true.

Chapter 35
Naomi
Christmas Day

Christmas day soon arrived, and Naomi was still unable to fully process what their grandma had been through, they wanted to make the day extra special for everyone.

Grandma Polly had felt tired and drowsy the last few days but after having some of her medication changed, she was feeling and looking a lot brighter.

"Merry Christmas grandma!" Naomi said as she gave her a kiss on the cheek.

"Merry Christmas love, don't you two look like the angel on top of a tree." Grandma gushed, complimenting the girl's dresses.

"Do you guys ever get jealous of us Aussies having a BBQ on the beach for Christmas, just out of curiosity?" Josh asked.

"That's actually real? I've always thought that was a myth." Naomi laughed feeling a bit jealous.

"Oh, it's true, it's something I've always wondered about you brits," Josh said sounding inquisitive.

"Well, I think you've got too much time on your hands." Mom laughed as she handed out the Bucks Fizz.

Just after dad and Stacey arrived everyone exchanged presents.

It really was a lovely morning filled with joy, happiness, and the relief of all being together again.

It wasn't long before mom had one too many sherries and let slip, she was seeing a man called Brian.

"I knew it, Katherine! See you can't fool me." Grandma said looking proud of herself.

"See now I'm jealous of the brits. That was beautiful Katherine, thank you so much!" Josh declared after clearing his plate and having seconds of all the turkey trimmings.

"Any time, Josh you can come again. I'm loving the compliments," mom chuckled.

"He's one big softy really," Clara said putting her arm around Josh.

The evening comprised of a game of charades, watching Eastenders and eating lots of Quality Streets chocolates.

Grandma went to bed about 9 and dad and Stacey left not long after.

"Right, I'm off to bed girlies, and Josh. Thank you all for a lovely day, it's been really special," mom said as she gave the twins a kiss on the head.

"Night mum," Naomi and Clara said at the same time.

It really had been a special day, the best Naomi thought.

Chapter 36
Naomi
May 2011

The next few months which followed that special day were tough.

Grandma Polly didn't have long left, and the family were told to prepare for the worse and say their goodbyes.

She was still Grandma Polly, but weaker and less chatty, which Naomi really missed.

She missed their endless chats and how one hour of talking soon became two.

But at the same time, she felt grateful. She was lucky to have such a strong, brave woman that she got the honour to call her grandma.

Clara was on her way down from Liverpool with Josh, and she just hoped she would make it in time to say goodbye.

The twin sisters had both agreed they needed to tell their mom the truth about everything that grandma had been through.

The night Naomi had told her, mom sobbed for hours. She felt guilty that she hadn't noticed but then she felt angry that it had been kept from her.

But eventually, she realised how brave her mom had been and that she had to do it to protect herself, and for that she was accepting of. Naomi's mom and grandma had talked about it privately and both women were glad it was out in the open and that grandma wasn't leaving with any secrets or regrets.

"Naomi, isn't it?" A voice behind Naomi said as she was staring blankly at a hospital board.

Naomi turned around to see a tall man in a doctor's uniform.

"Doctor Fabien. We met briefly just before Christmas when I dropped some flowers round for your grandmother. I'm very sorry to hear she isn't doing so well." He said looking sympathetic.

"Of course. Thank you, she loved those flowers by the way, really made her smile. It doesn't feel real if I'm being honest, but then I don't know what its meant to feel like." Naomi replied feeling deflated.

"Take a seat if you like," Doctor Fabien pointed to the waiting area chairs.

"There isn't a right or wrong way to feel. It's hard either way but I look at is as, feeling sad about it just shows how wonderful and special that person was. You can't say a right or wrong thing either because I'm sure your grandmother knows exactly how you're feeling without any words." Fabian said reassuringly.

"I think that might be one of the nicest things I've ever heard. There is something that's bugging me though," Naomi said knowing what she was going to say next, but not knowing why she was saying it.

"What's that?" Fabien asked.

"My grandmother had to give a child up for adoption when she was 16, through no choice of her own. These last few months I've had sleepless nights trying to find him. I know it sounds stupid, but I will just always think what if she could've seen him before she went, and then she'll know he's ok and she can leave peacefully. I know it probably sounds stupid, I'm sorry," Naomi said feeling embarrassed.

"Not at all. Don't apologise. I was adopted, I tried to find my birth parents a few years ago, but no luck unfortunately. The adoption records in Amsterdam aren't great, all I know from my adoptive parents is that I was originally called George." Fabien replied, looking disappointed.

Naomi couldn't believe what she had just heard. It couldn't be could it, she thought.

"You are going to think I sound crazy, but my grandmother had her son in Amsterdam and called him George in June 1941. She was forced to give him up for adoption because her partner Geoff got sent to a concentration camp for being Jewish, at least that's what she has always thought." Naomi said, the words falling out of her mouth hundred miles per hour.

"I will celebrate my 70th birthday next month. But surly this can't be real. I have a lemon-coloured blanket which I was told had been knitted by my maternal grandmother, it's in my briefcase I've always carried it with me, it got me through med school." Fabien said scrambling in his bag and pulling out a worn but noticeable knitted blanket.
"My grandma never mentioned that but stay here and I'll go and ask, oh I hope she's awake." Naomi said rushing off to her grandma's bed.

"What's the rush love, is everything ok?" Mom asked looking concerned.

"I just need to speak to grandma, is she awake?" Naomi said sounding out of breath.

"Yes, I'm just going to get her a cup of tea, I won't be long." Mom responded looking tired.

"Hi grandma," Naomi said feeling nervous.

"Oh, hello love, I thought you'd gone. Are you ok, you look very pale?" Grandma asked focusing on the funny complexion of Naomi's face.

"Did your mother knit anything for your son George when he was born?" Naomi asked feeling hopeful.

"Ummm yes, she did a little blanket to wrap him in when he was taken. I think, oh my brains a bit muddled but I'm sure it was a lemony colour. Why?" Grandma asked trying to think back to that day with joy and sadness at the same time.

"Oh wow, this is going to sound crazy grandma and I really don't want to upset you, but I think I've found him, or he's found us. I'm not really sure but I think I've found George!" Naomi said, as soon as the words left her mouth though, she was worried she was wrong because there was so much joy on her grandma's face.
"Mom?" Doctor Fabien entered Grandma Polly's hospital room.

"Doctor Fabien?" Grandma asked looking confused.

"Grandma, I think this is George. He was adopted in Amsterdam June 1941; he was told his birth mother called him George and…" Naomi said before she couldn't speak anymore.

"I have this, the lemon blanket knitted for me by your mother. I've had it with me every day. I tried to find you but…." George said holding back tears.

"You have his eyes. You have your fathers' eyes. Oh, my boy." Grandma wrapped her hands around George's face and pulled him in for a hug she had been waiting for, for 70 years.

Naomi left her grandma, mom, and George to all catch up while she went to meet Clara at the train station.

"Maybe she needed to be reunited with him before she you know goes. Maybe there is a reason he was under her care after all. Well done sis. I'm so happy for grandma, I'm just dreading saying goodbye." Clara said after Naomi had updated her on the walk to the hospital.

Chapter 37
Naomi

Two days later Grandma Polly took her last breath. She was surrounded by Naomi, Clara, Katherine, and George.

All four of them were at her bedside to say goodbye and make sure she was comfortable.

George was sad that he hadn't found her sooner or realised for that matter, but he was so grateful that they finally found each other again and he was able to hear all about his birth father as well.

Naomi and Clara had both cried for hours after, and a few days to come but they supported each other and kept telling themselves that a life well lived is a life well loved.

They knew their grandmother was happy in the end and that she would live on in their memories.

Mom had decided to do a buffet to get everyone together and have some fun which Grandma Polly insisted on.

Dad and Stacey came with their new-born Freddy and Brian joined, who was lovely and had really supported mom through these last few months, he had also had grandma's approval.

And of course, George joined them. Mom loved having an older brother and he very much enjoyed having a sister. They said their connection was automatic and it was like they'd never been apart.

Clara was still enjoying university and her and Josh were stronger than ever. As for Naomi, she enjoyed learning about law, but she'd also got into writing lately. Maybe she'll write a book in dedication to her wonderful grandmother, she thought.

The End

Printed in Great Britain
by Amazon

83062331R00098